The Thief
from Five Points

L. Travis teaches English at a Minnesota college and lectures frequently on fantasy and literature.

Ben and Zack Series, Book 2

The Thief from Five Points

L. Travis

BakerBooks

A Division of Baker Book House Co
Grand Rapids, Michigan 49516

© 1995 by L. Travis

Published by Baker Books
a division of Baker Book House Company
P.O. Box 6287, Grand Rapids, MI 49516-6287

Printed in the United States of America

Library of Congress Cataloging-in-Publication Data

Travis, L., 1931–
   The thief from Five Points / L. Travis.
     p. cm.   (Ben and Zack series ; bk. 2)
   Summary: While staying at his uncle's mission in New York
City during the Civil War, twelve-year-old Ben and his friend
Zack try to help a young girl escape from a gang.
   ISBN: 0-8010-8916-6
   1. New York (N.Y.)—History—Civil War, 1861–1865—Juvenile
fiction. [1. New York (N.Y.)—History—Civil War, 1861–1865—
Fiction. 2. Adventure and adventurers—Fiction. 3. Missions—
New York (N.Y.)—Fiction. 4. Gangs—Fiction.] I. Title. II. Series:
Travis, Lucille, 1931–   Ben and Zack series ; bk. 2.
PZ7.T68915Th   1995
[Fic]—dc20   94–27061

To Bryan with love
and thanks for bringing
Five Points to my attention

Contents

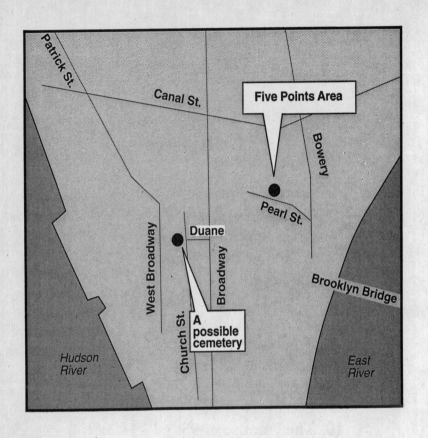

Patrick St.

Canal St.

Five Points Area

Bowery

Pearl St.

West Broadway

Duane

Broadway

Church St.

A possible cemetery

Brooklyn Bridge

Hudson River

East River

Things to Come

In the woods outside the village of Tarrytown, New York, two figures hunched behind a large tree. Ben never saw the two until they rushed at him with a force that knocked him to the ground.

"Copperhead!" Jeff Sorley stood above him shaking his fist in Ben's face. "Don't your pa know we got a war going on between us Northerners and those slave-owning Southerners? It wasn't too smart of your pa to help out that Southern woman last summer, now, was it? Hear tell he's preaching we ought to pray for the Southern boys fighting against our men. You tell your pa anybody who helps a Southerner is a low-down copperhead and worse than a snake. Your kind ain't welcome here in the North."

Ben tried to sit up, but Jake pushed him back hard with his foot. Ben gritted his teeth. He knew as much as Jeff Sorley about the war. The Northern states, called the Union, and the slave-holding Southern states, who called themselves the Confederacy, had been fighting for two years now, right into the winter of 1863. The battles between the Union army and the Confederate army raged outside of New York State, but the war had brought troubles here, too.

Though his pa was no copperhead, some Northerners did belong to a secret society that supported the South's cause. They were called copperheads after the lapel pin they wore, a head of liberty cut from a copper penny. Nowadays anyone caught supporting the enemy, the South, could be punished by imprisonment.

The younger Sorley spit close to Ben's head. "The way you run around with that Negro boy, Zack, a body would think you were an abolitionist instead of a copperhead. Ain't that funny, Jeff? A copperhead and an abolitionist in the same family."

Ben glared at the boy. Some folks blamed the war on the abolitionists, who took a hard stand against slave-owning and demanded that all slavery be done away with. Abolitionists were about as popular as poisonous snakes to a lot of folks up north who were willing to allow the South to keep slavery so that the war would end and the South would come back into the Union. Anger welled up inside Ben. He didn't need to be called an abolitionist to hate slave owning, and his pa wasn't a copperhead.

Deliberately the younger Sorley picked up a fistful of stones which he let loose at Ben. One of the larger stones struck Ben's eye and blinded him with pain. Covering his face with his arms, Ben rolled on his side. At the same moment he heard the deep baying of a hound and a familiar voice shouting nearby.

"Hey, what's goin' on?" Zack was running toward him with his uncle's old hound dog, Moss, racing ahead.

Startled, the attackers took off. Just before they disappeared into the woods, Jeff Sorley shouted back threateningly, "Copperhead."

"You okay, Ben?" Zack's black face glistened with sweat as he reached down to give Ben a hand.

"I'm okay," Ben muttered, "thanks to you and Moss." He pulled himself up from the damp ground.

Zack patted the dog's head. "She may be old, but she tracks good, and she sure is powerful loud. Bet those two still be running." He stared at Ben's face. "You look like we should've come sooner."

Ben carefully touched the tender skin around his left eye where the stone had hit. It felt swollen. "I guess it shows?" he asked halfheartedly.

"Yup," Zack agreed. "Too bad the rest of you ain't black, 'cause that eye sure is gonna be." He smiled knowingly. "You won't be hidin' that one from your ma."

Ben shoved his books under his arm. "I've got to do something, Zack. Just can't figure what. Ever since last summer, rumors that Pa is a copperhead have been going around town."

Zack raised an eyebrow. "Mistress Capp sayin' folks 'round here is gettin' wore out over this war, ready to blame anyone soon's a rumor starts," he said. Zack boarded with old Mistress Capp in exchange for doing her chores.

"Rumors have been thicker than flies lately," Ben agreed.

Zack shook his head. "Some folks spoiling for a fight, Ben, like them Sorley boys. Right or wrong, they ain't of a mind to care." Zack's dark eyes looked steadily at Ben. "You know your pa's no copperhead. Maybe we be dead now if it weren't for that Southern woman savin' our skins last summer and seein' we got home safe. To give her a head start before the marshal found out who she was weren't no more than a body ought to do." He leaned down to pat the dog who sat at his feet. "Maybe she was some kind of spy, but I'm plum sorry she never had the chance to go back home before somebody shot her." He lifted his head and looked at Ben. "You reckon by the time we come back from New York City things 'round here will settle down?"

A faint hope replaced the anger inside Ben. In a week they would leave Tarrytown for a whole month in New York City. Zack was going too. Pa was to be one of the preachers for the coming rally in the city to celebrate President Lincoln's Emancipation Proclamation, the order to free the slaves. That ought to show people Pa was no copperhead. Ben brushed the dirt from his hands. The sooner they left Tarrytown the better.

His eye had begun to sting. "Better be going home," he said. "You coming, Zack?"

Zack nodded. "Come on, Moss, let's go." Obediently the dog padded after the boys. Zack's long legs swung into an even pace with Ben's. The two of them were almost equal in height and weight. Twelve years old and growing like a couple of lanky colts, Ben's ma said, all feet and elbows.

Ben glanced at his friend. Zack was lost in thought.

"Ben, you reckon they'll be trouble in the city?" Zack asked.

Ben stood still and looked hard at Zack. "Are you thinking about last summer?" The memory of the July riots in New York City flashed through his mind. Angry mobs of whites had protested the war and the new draft laws by burning and looting, especially the section of the city where colored folks lived.

"You'll be safe with us, Zack," he said softly. "Pa says nothing like last summer could ever happen again in New York."

Zack looked away for a moment. "Reckon I ain't afraid."

They walked the rest of the way in a companionable silence, each caught up in his own visions.

Neither could have imagined the slight figure of a girl wrapped in a thick shawl as she hurried through a dark alley in a part of New York City known as the Five Points. Small in area, it was one of the worst slums of the times. It was crowded with the city's poorest, most of them immigrants, many from Ireland. The alley through which the girl ran ended next to a decaying building with worn steps that led down to a cellar. She descended and groped in the dark until she felt the wooden door before her. With a sharp rap she knocked four times and called in a low voice, "It's me—Letti. Open this door, Nat, and be quick about it." The door opened a crack, and Letti pushed her way inside.

A young boy dressed in a ragged coat too large for him and a shiny stovepipe hat atop a mass of straw-colored, uncombed curls held out a grimy hand. "Did you bring somethin' to eat? I'm near to starvin'," he said.

Letti loosened the shawl from her head and stood with her hands on her hips. Her own thick braids were the same straw color as her brother's curls. Her blue eyes, identical to his, snapped with disapproval. "You look like one of the Plug Ugly gang with that hat." She unwrapped a small bundle and held out its contents. "I brung what I could: leftover beef pie and pudding. But this has to be the last time. You've got to turn yourself in to the mission like I did, Nat, or there's no telling where you'll end up."

"Now don't start your nagging. Sister or no sister, I ain't about to listen to no preaching. Soon's I get work I won't need no help."

A few minutes later Letti left, closing the door behind her. Nat settled down on his rag bed to eat. He chuckled to himself. "Guess I do look like a Plug Ugly, seeing as how I aim to be one." Once he became an official member of the gang his worries would be over. He would learn to steal with the best of them. He already knew a few tricks from Letti. Hadn't she herself been one of the best thieves on the waterfront before that mission got hold of her? And why shouldn't he join the gang? Folks in the Five Points barely kept alive on the little they could earn. The Plug Uglies gang was tough. He'd do okay with them.

Nat finished the last of his beef pie. Pleased with himself, he chuckled again. Had he known how soon things were to change in his life and Letti's with the coming of Ben and Zack, he might have been terrified.

1
River Rats

"Whoa, I say." The driver's voice rose above the noise of the city street as he pulled back heavily on the reins. Within inches of colliding head-on with the horses of a large coach called an omnibus, they came to a standstill. The horses whinnied nervously.

"That was close," Ben said, leaning back from the window.

His mother frowned. "I don't think I want to know what it was we didn't hit this time," she said.

Silently Zack grinned at Ben. This was the second time the coachman had come near to tangling with the city traffic.

In the broad street an endless stream of horses, carts, coaches, and people struggled for the right-of-way. Newsboys in tattered jackets and worn shoes called out the evening headlines: "Locomotive plows into snowbank. Engineer killed. Cold closes Mississippi rail."

In spite of the shortages the war had caused, New York glittered in its holiday wear. Gentlemen in top hats and heavy coats, and ladies in hoop skirts, stylish capes, and furs hurried past in the cold. Christ-

16

mas wreaths and displays filled elegant store windows. Even the rooftops and iron-railing fences were decked with snow like thick white frosting. Bells on the horses' harnesses jingled merrily, and steam rose from their warm breath in the cold air. Ben could feel the excitement of city life everywhere around them.

They turned off onto a quieter street and within a few blocks entered a modest neighborhood. Here small, well kept houses held glowing candles in the windows, and Christmas wreaths hung on the doors. Snow-covered trees glistened in the light of tall lampposts.

Ben wondered how big his Aunt Hett's house would be. He remembered his aunt and uncle a little from the time before they had gone abroad. He could scarcely recall his cousin Abigail, who was thirteen, a year older than he. He had never seen the youngest girl cousin who would be about three years old.

Ben's mother tapped his knee lightly. "We should be at Aunt Hett's soon," she said, "and then you boys will get to stretch your legs. I declare mine are quite numb." Ben liked the way his mother included Zack. After his granny's death Zack had become like part of the family when he wasn't working for Mistress Capp.

His mother lifted the picnic basket on her lap, then lost her hold as the coach flung her small frame against Ben's father.

"Sorry, dearest," she said. "That wasn't meant to get your attention."

"Was I woolgathering?" Ben's father asked as he retrieved the basket.

His mother smiled. "Only for the last hour or so."

"Was it so long?" Tall and thin, he had been sitting hunched over, lost in thought. He sat up and straightened to his full height. "These coaches weren't made for a man my size."

A flash of pride went through Ben. His father was as tall as President Lincoln.

"Try to forget things for a little while, dear," his mother said. A note of weariness was in her voice.

Ben knew what she meant. The rumors that his father was secretly a copperhead had divided the Tarrytown church members into two groups. One group supported his father, but the others worried what the rumors might do to the church. He wished they never had to go back to Tarrytown or that the war would end and his father could go on being the minister the way he used to be, cheerful and respected by the townsfolk.

"Whoa, whoa," the driver commanded, bringing the coach to a jolting halt. Ben touched Zack's shoulder. This was it. With a sigh he climbed down after his folks. Zack was close behind him.

His aunt was there to greet them. Her short round person was wrapped in a long woolen shawl. Curly wisps of brown hair framed her girlish face. Ben's mother threw her arms around her sister and hugged her tightly. Then Ben, too, was enveloped in his aunt's arms.

Her breath came in little puffs as she spoke, "Oh,

Ben, you look so like your father." She took him by the arm and drew him toward a tall, thin girl with freckles on her nose and bright red hair. "Meet your cousin Abigail," she said cheerily.

Awkwardly Ben shook his cousin's hand and let it go almost at once.

Abigail smiled politely. Her deep blue eyes coolly judged him.

Feeling a small tug on his coat, Ben looked down. A dark-haired little girl stood at his knee. She clung to a worn, velvety toy rabbit. "Ben?" she said.

Her mother caught up the child in her arms. "Susie, this is your cousin Ben. And this must be his friend, Zack. Say hello, dear."

The little girl stared at Zack, who smiled a slow wide smile. "Is he always black, Mummy?" she asked.

"Why of course, dear, just as you're always white, the way God made each of you," Ben's aunt said. "Enough questions. Now inside with you before we all catch our death."

Like a mother hen, Aunt Hett shooed them through the hallway. "You boys will sleep in the attic," she said.

"Yes, ma'am!" Ben almost shouted. The attic sounded perfect—far enough away so that he and Zack could make their own plans.

A good fire blazed in the large sitting room where Zack and Ben waited till supper was ready. The delicious smell that came from the kitchen was of meat pies and something like cinnamon apples and made the house feel warm and welcoming. Ben's stomach growled as the odors of cooking grew stronger.

With great strides Uncle Hiram entered the room and nodded at the boys. A tall giant of a man with a thick, red, bushy beard, he towered above them. In one huge hand he held a large pocket watch. With a glance at the watch he announced in a booming voice, "Glad to have you, boys. We sit down to supper in exactly five minutes. Washroom's alongside the kitchen—can't miss it. Be on time, sirs."

Ben and Zack moved toward the kitchen instantly. The kitchen fire cast a soft glow on its simple furnishings. Leaning over a wooden table, a serving girl not much older than Ben and Zack ladled milk from a large milk can. Thick braids of straw-colored hair hung over her shoulders. Her face was rosy from the heat and her eyes were wary as she looked at Ben and Zack.

"The washroom?" Ben asked.

The girl didn't smile but pointed toward a door on her left. "Out back."

Zack finished drying his face, then patted his tightly curled black hair into place. "Ain't no way that girl's gonna let me in her kitchen."

"What are you talking about, Zack? You and me are sleeping in the attic." Back home Zack slept behind the wood box in Mistress Capp's kitchen, but here it would be different.

Zack shook his head impatiently. "I mean that girl don't want no colored boy at her table."

Ben threw the towel over its wooden peg. "Hang

it all, that can't be so in this house, Zack, not with my aunt and uncle. But if it comes to that we can both eat in the kitchen."

The sound of a large tin cowbell and the bellowing voice of his uncle startled Ben to action. His uncle still held the watch in his hand. "Punctuality, young men, is a virtue." With a snap he closed the watch and sat down at the head of the table.

To Ben's utter astonishment Aunt Hett guided Zack to the chair next to Ben at the foot of the table. At that moment the serving girl entered with a steaming platter, placed it in front of his uncle, and sat down beside Ben's cousin Abigail. Never before had Ben seen a serving girl sit at the table with her mistress and master.

At Ben's side, Zack sat as still as death. The only white man's table Zack had ever eaten at was Ben's back home in the parsonage. Ben knew that his own family was different from most other folks even in the North.

The serving girl kept her eyes downcast. Ben looked at his cousin Abigail. Her blue eyes stared straight at Ben; a look of defiance was on her face.

His uncle began to say grace. "We come before thee, Lord, as thy people, thy sheep, thy lambs, and we thank thee for thy provisions. Amen." Almost immediately Ben's father and uncle began an earnest conversation between bites of food. His mother and aunt at once fell to discussing things they had waited to tell each other. At Ben's end of the table the business of eating took over.

In a voice meant only for Ben to hear, Zack whispered, "Beats all. I thought only Quaker folk do like this, setting down with colored folk."

"Not only Quakers. Some folks like us think everyone should be treated fairly," Abigail said loudly.

"And I wish that everyone in New York thought the same," her father added. "But I'm afraid people in the city are not much different from the folks back in Tarrytown when it comes to treating their fellow human beings rightly. You can be sure that in this house you are a welcome guest, Zack."

"Thank you, sir," Zack said in a low voice.

Uncle Hiram waved the spoon in his hand like a banner. "You mark my words, lads, President Lincoln is a great leader. A new day is coming for this nation. One with freedom for all."

"Amen," Ben's father added. The two men went on speaking together in lowered tones.

"Letti, will you bring the apple pies now, please," Aunt Hett said. At once the serving girl rose and went into the kitchen. A second later the sound of crashing glass and Letti's scream brought everyone to their feet.

The girl rushed into the dining room holding in her hands a rock with a piece of paper tied to it. "Oh, ma'am, the kitchen window is all cracked and broken," she cried.

In a flash Ben's father and uncle hurried to the back door and flung it open. "Cowards, rock-throw-ing cowards," his uncle roared. "Come out and face me like a man, if there's a man in the lot of you."

"Be careful, Hiram," Aunt Hett called anxiously as the two men went out into the yard. She reached for the rock in Letti's shaking hand.

"What on earth is going on?" Ben's mother asked. "Who would throw a rock through your window? Is that a note attached to it?"

Aunt Hett held the paper up to read it: "Dirty abolitionists. Your kind ain't wanted here." The paper trembled in her hand.

"Oh, ma'am, they know I'm here, and it's no use." Letti covered her face with her hands.

"Now Letti, it could be anyone."

"No, ma'am. They're jealous and hate me for living here where you're all so good to me." Tears of anger flowed down Letti's face. "It's them River Rats I used to run with. I brung this trouble on you."

"Letti, it's a fact that we are against slavery in every way. And that makes us a target for some folks. But no matter what your old gang is up to, you belong here now." She patted Letti's shoulder. "This family stands up for what we believe. Just remember that."

Letti dabbed at her eyes with a corner of her apron. "Yes ma'am."

It was late, and Ben's eyes were growing heavy as he and Zack climbed the attic stairs. A small nightstand wedged between the beds held the candle. Ben hung his clothes on a wooden wall peg next to Zack's.

The bed was cold, but his aunt's feather comforters were thick. With the candle out, he lay listening to the unfamiliar sounds of the house creaking.

Breaking the silence, Zack said, "Could be bad trouble, Ben, if that River Rat gang find out your folks got a colored boy staying here."

Ben thought about it for a minute. "A mean rat is mean about everything, I guess."

"Maybe so," Zack agreed, "but we ain't back home, and I got a feeling city rats may be a whole different kind than small-town rats."

"There's more than one way to trap a rat, even a pack of them," Ben replied. "First thing in the morning we'll have a look around and find out more about Letti's old friends." In his mind Ben felt a nagging uneasiness. What were he and Zack getting into? Tomorrow he would find out.

Zack curled himself into a ball to keep warm. Back home the trouble was copperheads. Here Ben's uncle and his family were being called abolitionists. How many other white families in this city were like Ben's?

Zack pulled the thick blankets close. He missed the warmth of the old woodstove in Mistress Capp's kitchen, the night sounds of hot coals falling and wood hissing. He missed her nightly prayer, "The Lord is my shepherd. . . ."

2
A Strange Disappearance

Ben half listened to his mother's words. The other half of him was trying to find a way out so that he and Zack could carry on their own plans.

"New York City is a big place," his mother said. Her thickly lashed gray eyes were wide and serious. "Until you know your way around a bit, it won't hurt you to go with your Aunt Hett. Besides, she really needs you boys and Abigail to help her this morning. I promised I'd stay with Susie, and Letti feels like she's coming down with a cold. She certainly shouldn't go in this weather." His mother's tone was firm. "You two had better bundle up well before you go out."

Ben looked glumly at Zack. They would have to help his aunt.

It was more than plain cold out. A bitter north wind whipped down the street as he and Zack turned the corner. Ahead of them Aunt Hett and Abigail battled their billowing skirts while they steadied the large pot of soup they carried between them. Ben shifted his packages so that his face was partly protected.

Within a few blocks the neighborhood began to

change from modest homes to dilapidated buildings. As they walked on, the streets became narrower, the alleys between buildings darker. All at once they entered a crowded area where broken steps, dark dirty windows, rusted signs, and decay were everywhere. The tall, narrow buildings leaned close to one another, and some were built back-to-back. Piles of black snow stiff with refuse lay along the pitted and broken walkways. In the street, pigs driven by two boys with switches ran wildly past old carts and poorly dressed children. Zack moved out of the way as a fat sow swerved into his path to dig her nose into the frozen garbage. With a whack of his stick, one of the boys drove her into the street, which made the sow oink loudly.

Ben had stepped back against an iron fence railing to let the pigs pass. As he did, a ragged child with a tin pail clutched in one hand clambered from a dark doorway below the sidewalk level. Behind her a sharp voice called, "Don't you forget to fill the growler this time, my pretty, or you'll answer for it." The child hurried onto the sidewalk and past Ben. A ragged shawl covered her head and shoulders and thin dress, but the girl's feet were bare.

Ben's own feet inside his leather boots were cold from the long walk. How could that small girl not feel the cold? Together with Zack he hurried after his aunt. By the time they reached the right tenement building and entered its dark, cold hallway, Ben had seen other children wearing no shoes or wearing what barely passed for shoes. Some had rags wrapped around their feet. A few wore worn boots that looked sizes too big.

"Now, boys, you stay close and mind the steps," Aunt Hett said as she led the way. The windowless hall was dark. A foul smell hung in the air, as if animals and people and garbage odors had all mixed together on the floors and walls. The creaking wooden steps felt worn and uneven as they stumbled up them, groping for a foothold. Ben worried that at any moment the two in front would come falling backward in the cavelike darkness.

On the first and second landing it was impossible to make out many of the closed doors that lined the corridors. Aunt Hett ignored these and continued to climb until they reached a smaller staircase to the attic.

At her third knock the attic door opened. "Oh, ma'am, it's yourself!" a girl of about five exclaimed. She pushed the door back to let them enter. The room was cold. On the floor in one corner near a small unlit stove a baby played with a bit of rag only slightly dirtier than her own clothes and face. A tangle-haired toddler watched with large, solemn eyes. From a low bed against the wall a woman raised her head. The skin on her face stretched taut against the bones; her fevered eyes looked at them anxiously. The woman shivered under the thin blanket and pile of rags that covered her. Cold air blew through cracks in the bare walls, and it was apparent that no fire had been lit in the room this morning.

Aunt Hett went immediately to the sick woman's side. "We heard you were feeling poorly, Mary. I've brought a little soup and a few things to make you more comfortable."

The woman, whose cheeks were wet with tears, turned her face toward Aunt Hett. "It won't be long till I'm gone. I know you'll take care of the children." She stopped to cough, and Aunt Hett raised her head until she could breathe once more. "I thank the Lord for the mission, and you his angel of mercy," the woman whispered as Aunt Hett gently laid her back against the bed.

Ben put his bundle on the floor and wondered what he should do next. He glanced at the rest of the room, noting its only furniture—a small kitchen table and wooden chair. A shelf nailed to the wall held a few dishes and cooking items. He could see nothing else besides the few rags the children played with.

Abigail was already setting out bowls of soup for the children. "Don't just stand there," she commanded. "Zack, can you start a fire? Coal's in your bag and matches on top with the kindling."

Zack jumped into action. "Yes'm. Lighting fires is my job. Back home, Mistress Capp give all that trouble to me." Quickly he laid coals in the waiting stove and arranged the bits of wood.

"And, you, come here and feed this baby. Yes, you, Ben." Abigail picked up the baby, settled her on the chair, and tied a rag sash first around her waist, then to the chair. "That ought to keep you from falling on your little nose," she said. "Here's the spoon, Ben. Just see that she doesn't get too much all at once and choke."

Gingerly Ben gripped the spoon and dipped it into the thick broth. The baby opened her mouth wide, and Ben fed her, wishing that he had stopped to wipe her runny nose first. He didn't dare now. Like a hungry little bird, the baby opened her mouth each time Ben brought the spoon near, again and again.

While the children ate soup, Zack's fire built to a warm glow. Water fetched from the pump in the courtyard soon bubbled in a tin pot. Quickly and expertly, Aunt Hett bathed the invalid mother, then tucked a new warm blanket about her. Abigail washed the children's faces and combed their hair. Warm woolen stockings, jackets, and shawls from Ben's packages soon transformed the little ones so that they were hardly recognizable as the same children he had first seen.

Abigail finished pinning a bright red bow on the five-year-old's hair. "Now then, Maggie, you're all set. There's bread and potatoes for tomorrow, and the rest of the soup. You be sure to cover the food in the tin box with the lid latched tight so the rats don't get at it."

"I'll do just that, ma'am," the child said. Her eyes sparkled with the promise of tomorrow's meal.

Aunt Hett took a last look at the fire and the

remaining coal. "Don't worry, Mary," she said. "Later today one of the missionaries will come by with the good doctor and bring more coal, too." She returned to her patient and picked up the frail hand in her own. "And now before we go, my dear, shall we sing your song?"

"Oh, please, if you would. It does my poor heart good to hear of the Savior, for I feel closer than ever to that shore."

Abigail joined her mother at the bedside, and together their voices blended in the sweet harmony of an old hymn, "There Is a Happy Land." Zack bowed his head as if in prayer, and Ben stood quietly listening. A lump formed in his throat. Never had he seen such misery as in this part of the city called Five Points.

On the way home Aunt Hett made one more stop. Opposite Five Points' fenced-in patch of dirt called Paradise Square, which Ben thought could have been more fittingly named the Devil's Pit, stood an imposing five-story building. Unlike its tottering neighbors it looked new.

"That's where the Old Brewery used to stand," Aunt Hett pointed out. "And beside it was Murderer's Alley. Before the mission bought the building and tore it down, the place was a den of thieves and drunkards and murderers. The new building has schoolrooms, clothing rooms, baths, kitchen, chapel, and a number of rooms for tenants in the upper floors." Aunt Hett opened the wide arched door. "But with thirty thousand homeless children in this city, and the poor packed into places like the Five Points, it's a small light in the dark, I'm afraid."

A sign over the archway said *The New York Tract Society*. The bright entryway and polished wood desk where the receptionist sat was a thousand times more cheerful than anything else Ben had seen so far in Five Points. The gentleman who greeted them ushered them to seats in the waiting room while Aunt Hett made arrangements for coal to be sent to the family they had just visited.

Abigail busied herself with a notebook she had brought with her, intently studying whatever was in it. Ben fidgeted with his cap, spinning it and then stopping it. He was just about to toss it to Zack when a policeman entered the door. His large hand firmly grasped a girl of eight or nine.

"Ouch. You let me go. I ain't done nothin'. You can't turn me in." The girl fought like a tomboy. Her bare feet kicked against the policeman's legs. From her thin dress and ragged shawl two dirty arms flailed against his chest. Her black hair flew in a tangled mass that had probably never felt a comb or a brush.

The policeman kept his grip on her arm. "Here you be, Mr. Blarney. Another one for Matron. Her name is Molly, and she's as wild a tyke as ever I've seen. No address, no family. We found her living inside an old burnt-out safe down near the docks. Half froze she was, though she's thawing out fast now." He grinned but still held onto the girl.

At a bell signal from Mr. Blarney the matron, a motherly looking woman in a starched white apron, appeared from a side room. She smiled, took the protesting child by the hand firmly, and led her away, speaking softly to her all the while.

Mr. Blarney the receptionist removed his glasses to wipe them. "Thank you, Officer Gallahan. She won't be the first child to come in like that nor the last, I fear. Never mind, we'll have the poor little thing looking like a princess; and with some nourishing food inside her, there's a good chance you won't know her for the same within a week."

"Well, and good day to you then," the officer said. "I expect you'll be sending your own orphans out west with the trainload that's leaving from the Children's Aid Society come New Year's Day?"

"Yes, indeed," the receptionist replied. "We plan on sending fifty children along. Though I much doubt she will be ready, maybe our new Molly will be one of them."

The officer left as Aunt Hett returned. Within a few minutes they were on their way home.

Ben was puzzled. Why was a trainload of orphans to be sent out west? How could that girl of eight or nine have no family at all? Where were they? "Beats all, doesn't it, Zack?" he whispered.

Zack thrust his hands into his pockets and lowered his head against the cold. "Reckon city folks got their share of problems."

At home the biggest problem yet waited. Ben's mother held Susie's hand, and her voice was anxious as she greeted them at the door. "Oh, Hett, it's terrible. Letti's gone. When I went upstairs to freshen up, I asked her to watch Susie and said I'd be right down. When I came back, Susie was in her chair playing with a doll, and Letti was gone. There's been no word or sign of her all day."

3

A Robbery

Ben followed his father through the narrow alley that led to Letti's old boardinghouse. Maybe they would find her here, but he doubted it. Who would want to stay in this place? The foul smell of the hallway reminded him of the tenement Aunt Hett had taken them to yesterday. He buried his nose in his muffler. More than likely, Zack and Uncle Hiram would find Letti down on the wharves where the River Rat gang hung out.

"Here it is, son, second floor, third door," his father said. He knocked lightly. For a moment there was no answer; then the door opened slightly.

"Wotch yer want?" The woman in the doorway eyed them suspiciously. Her face was defiant above her ragged dress and bare feet.

Ben's father answered cheerfully. "We were hoping to find a young girl named Letti, my sister-in-law's serving girl. My sister-in-law would very much like to have her back if she is willing to come."

The woman stepped aside. "See for yerself. She ain't here. Me and the mister's took this place goin' on two months, and ain't nobody else by that name."

The room before them was littered with piles of rags. Several thinly clad children sat at the piles sorting and shaking the dirty bits of cloth. There were no windows, and the air was thick with dust. In one corner two old men and an old woman worked at the heaping piles of rags in front of them.

The woman gestured toward the old people. "Them's our boarders. Don't none of them have no children. Just rents out a bit of the room to work and sleep in."

Ben stared at the littered floor, the gaping cracks in the grime-covered walls, the packing boxes that served as furniture, and the small stove. The children paused in their work and watched him with a hungry look in their eyes.

Back in the dark hall once more, Ben's father went first down the narrow, worn stairs. Outside they walked quickly. His father's long legs strode past the mounds of slop, the litter, and the figures huddled in doorways to escape the cold. In the street and on the walk, it seemed to Ben, they were the only two who were warmly dressed in this place of beggars, drunkards, fierce-looking people, and ragged children. Ben hurried to keep up with his father.

At supper an uneasy quiet hung over them all. There was still no word of Letti's whereabouts. Uncle Hiram and Zack had searched everywhere without success. Abigail, whose eyes were telltale red, said nothing. Only Susie prattled on, mostly to Zack, her new favorite, who patiently answered her constant questions.

Ben's father looked thoughtful as he set his cup down. "Hiram, what we saw this afternoon in the Five Points haunts me."

"And well it should, Stewart," his uncle said. "I'm not surprised that you can't get the taste of that place out of your mouth. Neither could I the first time I visited there. Why, man, there's not a worse slum anywhere." Both Ben and Zack jumped when his huge hand suddenly slapped against the table.

"It makes a man's blood boil. In that slum a single lot no bigger than twenty-five feet by one hundred feet is packed with two hundred eighty men, women, and children in hovels not fit for livestock."

Abigail fished a small abacus from her apron pocket, moved the beads quickly, and announced triumphantly, "Papa, that means one person every nine square feet."

"You must figure in the number of floors in a tenement building," her father said, "which will come out about the same space per person as it would if we had forty people living here in this house."

Ben thought that his uncle's house was crowded with the nine of them, if Letti were included. Thirty-one more people became unimaginable.

"And on Orange Street," Uncle Hiram said, "three thousand people live in a one-half-mile strip."

"But that's inhuman in this day and age," Ben's father protested.

Aunt Hett stopped clearing the table to add, "Yes, and worse still, in that same half mile on Orange Street you can count two hundred seventy saloons serving the vilest drink imaginable in every kind of den."

Ben's father nodded. "The miserable try to forget their misery, and the greedy take advantage of them by offering an escape that turns out to be a cruel slavery in the end."

"You say rightly when you say cruel," Ben's uncle added. "Many's the time we've seen a poor wife half-beaten to death, or the children bruised black and blue from both drunken parents."

Ben tried to picture in his mind what his uncle was saying.

"Or their very clothes, and little they have, sold for drink and gambling," Aunt Hett added.

Uncle Hiram cleared his throat. "We need laws to protect the children from those who sell them, work them to death, even starve them for their own profit." His voice had risen with anger.

Ben's aunt put her arms about her husband's neck, saying softly, "Now that we're here, Hiram, we can work for good laws. But we mustn't forget that only a few years ago missionaries couldn't enter the Five Points without a police escort for protection. The mission's work has made a real difference already, and it will grow."

"Well," Ben's father added, "for as long as we're here in the city I'd like to help out at the mission."

Ben felt a surge of pride for his father. His mother smiled her approval.

His uncle nodded. "There's plenty of work, Stewart. You will find that out soon enough. The hungry come to be fed, the ragged to be clothed, the children to be taught, the sick to be helped, and the devil's own to try and stop us."

"Then it's settled. I'll do what I can to help, that is, if they'll have me."

"Have you?" Uncle Hiram roared. "With the cold spell a week long, half the volunteer staff's laid up with sore throats and fevers."

"Beats all," Zack muttered as they followed the family to the sitting room, where the men settled down to read and the women to sew. Abigail had already left with Susie to put her to bed. Ben picked up the game he and Zack had started earlier.

Bent over her knitting, Aunt Hett fretted. "I ought to have spoken with the child before she took it into her mind to leave us. Poor thing somewhere out there in the cold." She sniffed and dabbed at her eyes with a hanky.

Uncle Hiram laid down his newspaper. "Now, Mother, don't you worry. The Lord will take care of his lamb. Tomorrow I'll go down to the police station and see if any word has come in."

The following day dawned clear, cold, but windless. After lunch Aunt Hett came downstairs with an armful of mufflers. "There's no sense in you children sitting around this house. What you need is some fresh air. I think it's high time you went skating. In this cold the ice in Central Park must go clear to the bottom of the lake."

Ben looked at Zack. Going with his cousin wasn't what he had planned. What if she couldn't skate? The picture of Abigail with her ankles buckling and her feet sliding from under her made him laugh out loud. Zack looked puzzled.

Bundled to their chins, the three waited for the horses pulling the omnibus to slow to a stop. Abigail pointed to the small red flag in its front window. "They always carry a red flag when the ice is safe enough for skaters," she said knowingly as they boarded.

Ben paid the six-cent fare and led the way to a seat near the front, where they could watch the spectacle of horsemen, buses, carts, and pedestrians juggling for the right of way. The ride uptown took them past great clothing stores with decorated windows, magnificent marble buildings, hotels, and high-class restaurants that made Ben wish they had walked. There was so much to see.

At Fifth Avenue the bus turned off Broadway and headed north for the 59th Street gate to Central Park. As Ben stepped down from the bus he saw Zack reach out a hand to pat the nose of one of the horses who whinnied back at him. There was no such thing as a horse that didn't get along well with Zack. Abigail had noticed, too, and flashed an admiring smile at Zack.

Inside the park the large lake stretched clear and smooth ahead of them, its ice glittering in the sunlight. Two yellow signposts announced an evening costume skating party to be held by torchlight, and Ben saw that a few skaters already wore costumes. He grinned as a man in a heavy brown bear outfit waddled by as his ankles turned in badly.

On ice Ben felt like he was in a different world, free, alone, and yet not alone. He knew he was a good skater, though Zack was quicker. They had raced one another on a frozen Tarrytown pond for the last five winters. He could tell in his bones that he would try again today and probably fail again to beat Zack. He was surprised and slightly miffed when Zack skated on ahead in a race with Abigail. Her ankles did not buckle, and she was fast. Her red hair flew from under her hood as she and Zack raced.

Three hours later when they caught the omnibus for home, Zack was still unbeaten. He and Abigail were deep in conversation about the infamous John Brown, the abolitionist executed for his raid on Harper's Ferry four years before. The two barely seemed aware of Ben until he suggested they ride partway and walk the rest past the holiday shop windows.

At the corner of Broadway and Grand Street in front of Messrs. Lord and Taylor's elegant store, Ben signaled to stop, and they left the bus. The huge store in its ornamented white marble building took up one hundred feet of Broadway and one hundred twenty-five feet of Grand Street, with windows all along the avenue side.

Suddenly Abigail gasped and grabbed Ben's arm. Not a block ahead on Grand Street in front of an empty cart stood Letti. Before any of them had time to move, a woman came out of the store, her arms full of bundles. At once Letti with her head down, walked straight toward her, and deliberately bumped hard into her.

"Oh, clumsy wretch!" the woman cried. "Just look at what you've done." Packages lay scattered on the walk. Hindered by her wide, fashionable hoop skirt, the woman bent to retrieve her bundles.

"Sorry, ma'am," Letti said loudly and stooped easily to scoop up two of the bundles. At that exact moment a small raggedly dressed boy darted from behind the cart, snatched the woman's purse, and ran up Grand Street. Stunned, Ben and the others watched the scene.

"Help! Help! Thief! Stop that boy! Someone stop him!" the woman shouted. In a flash, Letti sped away after the boy with two of the woman's packages under her arm.

People were beginning to come to the woman's aid. A stout gentleman waving his walking stick in the air chased after the thieves. In a moment, red-faced and out of breath, he stopped. Meanwhile the woman continued to shout, "Help! Someone catch them."

A shop clerk, coatless and hatless, hurried from

the store. He began to pick up the packages and exclaimed, "Oh dear, madam, I am so sorry!"

"Fool!" the woman cried. "Never mind those. Call the police." The poor man dropped what he held and hurried back into the shop. Others helped to pick up the now twice-dropped bundles.

"Such a dreadful state of affairs in this city," one onlooker commented as she brandished her fur, lined muff in the direction of the thieves. "And not a policeman in sight."

"Come on," Abigail shouted. "She's getting away." With her skates flopping on her shoulders, Abigail ran after the fleeing Letti, who had just turned off Grand Street onto Mercer.

As they rounded the corner Ben spotted Letti making her way toward the end of the street to what looked like a graveyard of charred, blackened houses. He saw her stoop down, then disappear through a break in the wooden wall that surrounded one of the ruins. "Over there!" Ben cried.

Zack and Abigail had seen Letti too. At the moment, the street was deserted, and without hesitation Ben crept into the narrow opening in the wooden wall.

Behind him Abigail stumbled through, followed by Zack. Bare broken beams and tumbled stonework stood before them. There was no sign of Letti or the boy in the deserted yard or outside the fence.

Abigail stopped looking and sat down on a wooden platform left behind by some workman. "This was the Chalmers' house," she said. "Last summer the rioters burnt it down along with the rest of the houses here. The rioters said they were taking revenge on the draft supporters, but the police claimed they did it just to loot the homes."

In the eerie silence of the ruined mansion the three sat on the old platform. After a minute Abigail threw her skates on the ground. Her red face was defiant. "I don't care if she does get caught and sent to prison at the Tombs. How could she go back to her old ways? The whole thing was a setup. That boy snatched the woman's purse while Letti got her attention. Then she ran off with two of the woman's packages. The old Letti used to do things like that." Abigail was close to tears. "We thought she'd changed."

Zack looked thoughtful. "My Grandpa Bell used to say if folks don't act like themselves, could be they got a heap of trouble. Sorta like when a horse shies away from somethin' in the grass. Makes no sense, lessen you know there's a rattlesnake in that grass. You reckon the River Rat gang's mixed up in this?"

"Could be so," Ben said. "Maybe Letti ran into them, and they forced her back with them."

"Well, I don't see how," Abigail argued. "Besides, she left the house in the middle of the day with no explanation, no note, or anything."

Ben stood to his feet. The afternoon light was starting to fade. "We can look around some, see which way they went out of here."

Halfheartedly Abigail picked up her skates and

got up. "Knowing Letti's past, I don't guess we'll find her or the boy. She can hide in a dozen places and make her way to Five Points."

Ben pulled his muffler more tightly about his neck. He was beginning to feel the cold. "We might as well take a look."

"No thanks." Abigail's face was as red as her hair. "I'm going home. You two can do what you like." She turned back toward the hole in the fence.

Zack looked at Ben and shrugged his shoulders. "I'm thinking we better go, too."

"It's okay with me," Ben said. He shouldered his skates. "I hardly know the girl."

In the darkening ruins two small shadows huddled inside an old brick oven where the mansion's summer kitchen had once stood. The boy fidgeted in the cramped space. Letti pushed him down against the hard floor. "You hush," she whispered menacingly, "or you'll get us both sent to the Tombs."

4

A School for Thieves

Dark had fallen when Letti finally led the way from their hiding place, back through the wooden fence, and out into the street. When at last they reached the Five Points, she and the boy hurried toward a certain shop. The rusty tobacco sign above the shop's unlit display window swung back and forth in the wind. Quickly the two made their way around to the back of the building. The boy stood shivering in the cold as Letti knocked three times on the heavy wooden back door.

From a small peephole an eye surveyed them; satisfied, its owner opened the door. The older boy who let them in held a long cigar between his teeth. "What took yer? Crimey, is that all you got?" he asked as he took the purse the boy handed him.

Letti held out her two packages. "The boy's new at snatching," she said. "He did just fine this last time," she added. She did not say that at three different stores the boy had failed to act on her signal and Letti had been unable to follow through on their planned thefts. "These ought to be worth something," she said cheerfully as the older boy took the packages.

"When do we eat?" the younger boy asked, beating his hands against his arms to warm them.

"Grub's inside. But I'm telling you, Marm ain't gonna like this. You two oughta had another purse at least by now."

"Couldn't help it," the boy said. "Had to hide out in the Chalmer's place till those kids left." Hunger and fear made him angry now, and turning on Letti he accused her. "How come that bunch of snobs knew your name anyhow?" Letti's face paled.

Roughly the older boy took Letti's arm before she could move. "What's this? You didn't tell me you were recognized. Slipping are you now? Suppose you go on in and explain to Marm."

Marm Mandlebaum, head of the city's largest ring of thieves and sole owner of her school for thieves, where the only subject taught was stealing, looked grim. Silently she counted the money in the purse the boy had snatched. "Mm, wife of one of our more comfortable gentlemen, I'll wager." Marm's own gown of fine winter stuff edged with velvet, and her furs, spoke of a certain comfort of her own. The packages each contained soft silks and lace of considerable value. "Well, is that all? You will have to work a little harder next time for your keep, eh?" She turned to look at the older boy. "My carriage is waiting. I think you can handle the rest for tonight, Jack." She looked at him with a frown.

"Right you are, Marm," he responded hastily. "But there's a small matter here you ought to know about." Marm listened first to Jack, then to a faltering Letti as she explained the circumstances that had made them late.

Marm's sharp eye took in Letti's appearance. Silent for a moment, she seemed lost in thought. "So you ran away from your benefactors back to the streets. You're a clever girl if you want to work for Marm. There's money in it for a girl who learns well, but I think now I may have misplaced you."

Her jeweled hand reached out to grasp Letti's chin and turn her face upward to the light. "Yes, dearie, perhaps the streets are not the only place for you. We've a whole school here with more advanced classes for our brighter girls. There's silver and rich pickings if you know where to look for them. We'll train you, get you hired out as a servant in a big house. You trust the rest to Marm." Marm's voice was low and persuasive. "Jack, put her in with Lizzie's class tomorrow morning."

She turned to the small boy and patted his head with a motherly hand. "As for you, we'll find another partner for you. Now run along and eat your supper. In Marm's school there's food for all."

Letti, still trembling with fear, followed her former partner into the hallway where another door led to a large room Marm called the schoolroom. Noise and laughter and the clanging of dishes greeted them as they opened the door.

Behind them Marm put a gloved hand on Jack's shoulder. "Don't let the girl out of your sight," she hissed. "She'll bear watching till she's in too deep to get out again. As for the boy, a few strokes of the rod ought to make him step lively next time." The cool, hard look in her eyes betrayed the fixed smile she gave Jack. "I trust you to see to it."

Inside the large room logs blazed in the huge fireplace. The smell of stew cooking wafted from two iron pots hung by the fire. Letti found a plate, helped herself to the mutton stew, bread, and ale, then looked carefully about for a place to eat.

The faces in the crowded room ranged from the very young to those her own age, with a few exceptions like Jack's. None of them was familiar. She hid her disappointment as she sat down next to a thin girl with long, stringy blonde hair. Sooner or later she would find some way of getting to Nat. Hungry, she ate quickly.

Marm was right about one thing—she did feed her pupils. Letti wondered, though, what happened when one of her students failed to bring in the required haul? She shivered in spite of the warm room and remembered how close she had come to bringing down Marm's wrath on her own head. Being recognized in the very act of lifting a customer's bundles was bad enough, but withholding information could be very dangerous. Well, there were some things she could tell no one.

Her whole body ached with tiredness and tenseness as she sat leaning against the wall and listened to the girl beside her. The talk was all about the latest fight between two rival gangs, the Dead Rabbits and the Bowery Boys. Letti pretended to yawn indifferently and casually asked if anyone had heard anything about the River Rats lately.

"Them? Same as always. They keep to their territory down on the waterfront so long's nobody tries to horn in, and them as does turns up floating in the river face down." The boy who spoke lit a cigar and blew little puffs of smoke into the air.

His companion, a lad of about ten, added, "Hear they caught the devil of River Rats himself, Jerry McCauley. They sent him up to Sing Sing Prison." Letti knew of the dreaded prison, one of the most feared places in New York.

The boy with the cigar looked disdainful. "Him? Why that's old news. Caught him so dead drunk he couldn't get away."

The man they spoke of was a dangerous thief who belonged to the older gang of River Rats. It was the younger gang, those Letti's own age, who interested her. For now what she wanted was information. She could not risk running up against the River Rats on her own. As long as she belonged to Marm's network of thieves she hoped to be safe, at least for the time being. Not many gangs would risk Marm's anger. Besides, it was well known that even the River Rats came to Marm to sell some of their own stolen goods.

The hour grew late, and most of the students bedded down for the night in the room that served as both classroom and inn. Letti rolled herself into her cape on the hard floor and closed her eyes. She would not let thoughts of Abigail or the soft bed she had left behind stay in her mind. "It's all I can do," she murmured to herself miserably.

Out in the hall someone was crying. As the door opened Letti glanced up. In the firelight she saw the young boy who had been her partner in crime for the day. He clutched his hands to his chest moaning softly. Behind him Jack entered with a thin rod in his hands.

Poor thing, Letti thought. That's the way of it. She knew. And Nat would know, too, if she didn't find him soon. Wearily she closed her eyes.

5

A Great Celebration

New Year's Day gripped the city in bitter cold. Giant icicles hung from snow-covered roofs. Swirls of frost coated every windowpane with designs. Outside in the frozen streets heavily loaded carts creaked by, their drivers huddled in blankets. From behind the morning newspaper Ben's father read aloud, "Two soldiers frozen to death at Island Number Ten. Three near Fort Pillow."

Aunt Hett clucked in sympathy. "It makes a body sad to think of it."

Ben's father read on: "Volunteers needed to knit five thousand pairs of mittens, says chairman of the Woman's Central Relief Association." He was more relaxed in the last few days than Ben had seen him for weeks. He glanced up with a teasing look at Aunt Hett. "That's a lot of knitting. Maybe you and Sarah ought to teach us men a stitch or two."

Ben started to laugh, but Zack said quietly, "Already know."

Before Ben could say, "But that's girl's stuff," Aunt Hett interrupted.

"Grandpa Boone could sew as good as any

woman, and he wasn't the first man, either. Any time you want to help out, Zack, just you let me know." Her round face beamed at Zack, who looked back shyly. "Meantime, you can all help serve a good hot meal to our soldiers and their families down at Hope Chapel this afternoon."

The large chapel was packed. At first, the sight of so many wounded, legless, or armless soldiers made Ben want to look away. It was the men themselves, with their cheers for President Lincoln and their courage, that helped him.

A uniformed soldier, whose right eye was covered and one arm still in bandages, took a clean plate from Ben. He was not much older looking than Ben's father. "Thank you, son," he said. "Appears like I have a lot to be thankful for, like the good folks at home here. There's a passel of boys back in winter camp on the Potomac haven't seen food like this for a month."

Ben nodded. "The paper's calling it the Union's Valley Forge," he said.

Someone down the line added, "The suffering this winter's been terrible—worst I ever seen. For every one man killed by the war there's two done in by sickness." Others agreed.

A man who stood next to the first soldier spoke in a low voice, "They say two hundred men a day are deserting."

Standing in line for a plate, a man with a wooden peg leg spoke up. "December's been a hard month all around. We lost 12,600 men at Fredricksburg. I heard old Burnside himself wept at Moray's Height. Our men made fourteen assaults. Nigh on to nine thousand of our own boys lost their lives there." The man took his plate from Ben with a half salute. "Couldn't hardly hold the general back from leading the next assault himself. Freezing cold then, too, I hear." The soldier moved ahead, and the sound of his wooden leg was lost in the general noise of the room.

For hours Ben passed out plates while Zack took empty ones back to the kitchen crew to wash. The crowd seemed endless. By late afternoon over a thousand people had eaten. But tired as he was, Ben felt good.

At five o'clock Aunt Hett and her crew finished their duties and left the chapel. Outside on Broadway carriages still carried New Year's Day visitors making their rounds of social calls. Crowded omnibuses hurried past; the horses' breath was white in the bitter cold. By the time they were able to hail a passing coach, Ben's feet were numb, and Zack had drawn his muffler up above his nose to keep warm. Abigail's face looked as red as her hair.

At home a welcome fire blazed in the sitting room fireplace. Ben's mother was taking fragrant mince pies from the kitchen oven. Like a small shadow, Susie tagged after her. "We just have time for a bite of supper before you leave for the meeting, Stewart," his mother said.

Inwardly Ben groaned. His father had come to

the city for this event. He had forgotten that he would have to go, as well as Zack and Uncle Hiram. One look at Zack's face was enough for him to stifle a complaint. Many famous men would be at the meeting tonight to celebrate what President Lincoln had done for the colored people. Still, Ben knew they would have to sit through speeches, probably like the ones the mayor and leaders of the town gave back home each Fourth of July. He frowned. Of course, here there would be no picnic and no fireworks afterward. A small sigh escaped him.

As if he had read Ben's thoughts, his father said, "Ben, you and Zack will see history made tonight. One day they'll call it the great ratification meeting of New York to celebrate President Lincoln's proclamation of liberty to the slaves." His voice held the same ringing note that Ben had often heard him use in the pulpit during a sermon. "I would like you both to pay your own way. Your twenty-five-cent admission fee will go to help educate Negro students at Wilberforce University, maybe even send books and teachers to the South, or provide reading materials for our colored troops. Agreed?"

"Agreed!" Zack almost shouted.

"I don't see why a woman can't go, too." Abigail spoke with a flash in her eyes and a toss of her red hair.

"In the first place, there wouldn't be room for all the women who'd like to go," Aunt Hett said, "and secondly, we women have three tickets to use tonight at the new Mammoth Stereoscopticon show, 'Mirror of the Universe.'"

Ben bit his tongue. He and Zack had seen the ads at Hope Chapel announcing the six-hundred-square-foot canvas screen that would be lit with a lamp as bright as noonday. The show promised to include something called "The White Lady, the Spirit of the Alps." "Seems like they could've had it on another night," he muttered.

"Ain't no account next to history," Zack retorted. He ignored Ben's questioning look.

Ben's mother sneezed before she could muffle it in her handkerchief.

"Are you sure you ought to go out in this cold air, my dear?" His father seldom noticed such things back home, but now, away from the cares of the church flock, he turned his full attention to his family.

"You know, Stewart," his mother sniffled and went on, "I wouldn't miss it for the world. Certainly not 'The White Lady of the Alps.' And Mrs. Potter is all set to mind Susie, so we women will just be off for a grand evening."

Ben did not laugh with the others. He would have traded places with any of the women. With a scowl he followed Zack to the washroom.

The Cooper Union building stood across the northern end of the Bowery section of the city. As they entered, Ben forgot his complaints for the moment. A wave of black faces smiling and talking filled the great hall. The warm smell of sweat and hair oil seemed friendly to Ben. Here and there white faces dotted the crowd, some with clerical collars around their necks. An usher took his father's arm and led them to seats reserved for the guest speakers and friends.

What all was said that night Ben couldn't really remember, but he would never forget the overwhelming feeling of joy and energy everywhere around him. When his father finished his speech Ben clapped till his hands burned. Other speakers followed until it was finally the turn of Senator Sumner, the main speaker.

As the senator ended his moving speech, the whole room erupted in cheers first for President Lincoln, then for the valiant men who defended the Union. Zack stood cheering with the rest at the top of his lungs, and Ben beside him did the same. Some of the men on the platform who had once been slaves and were now free men wept openly. Ben could see tears on the faces of men all around him. At the end, every man in the hall stood to sing together as with one mighty voice the new song "The Battle Hymn of the Republic." Ben thought his heart would burst with pride.

It was afterward that grim reality thrust itself before them. At the close of the meeting some folks lingered to talk. Ben and Zack stood waiting while Ben's father and uncle greeted friends. The talking went on and on as others filed out. Ben had grown impatient when an unexpected commotion at the door caught his attention.

A young colored man, his face bloodied and his coat torn, limped into the hall. Angry voices rose but were suddenly hushed as a tall figure in uniform approached the men gathering around. Ben knew the imposing gentleman in military dress. He was one of the guests of honor, Chaplain H. M. Turner, the first commissioned Negro chaplain in the United States Army. Others respectfully drew back for him.

"What happened, son?" he asked.

"I left the hall to walk back to Prince Street, sir," the young man said, still breathing hard. "They are housing and feeding some of us who are visitors down at Kinny's Hall on Prince Street. Well, I sure didn't get far before two white men grabbed hold and started beating me. Guess they didn't count on me being cold sober and a lot quicker on my feet, sir." He smiled. "I ran back here mighty fast. Reckon it might do to join up with a few of the brethren going my way." At that several voices offered him an escort.

The chaplain laid a gloved hand on the young man's shoulder. "Don't mistake the whole city for the rabble who'd prey on any man, black or white. By the way, son, if you're thinking about the army, we can use men like you. Just you say I sent you."

As the crowd once more began to make its way out, Ben followed his father and uncle to the exit. Zack seemed unaware they were leaving, and Ben tugged at his arm. "Come on, Zack. You look out or you'll never find us in this mob." He held firmly to Zack's sleeve on their way toward the door. "I think if somebody asked you right now, you'd sign up, too," he said.

"Reckon if he asked, I would," Zack said.

6

Trouble in Five Points

During the night Ben awakened as he felt the cold air of the attic on his bare chest. He had been dreaming that he was following Zack in a line of soldiers marching across a frozen field toward the enemy. Still groggy with sleep, Ben reached for his blanket, which had slipped to the floor. As he wrapped it tightly around him he heard the sounds of hurrying footsteps and whispering voices. What was going on downstairs? Had Letti come back?

A light from the hall below shone dimly through the open attic doorway. Quietly he brushed past the hulk of blanket that was Zack asleep with the quilt pulled over his head. From the top of the stairs Ben could hear a deep, painful sound of coughing that came from his parents' room.

Aunt Hett hurried down the hallway with a large pitcher and towels. She paused to look up at Ben. "Now, dearie, don't you fret. Everything's under control here." Quickly she disappeared into the guest room.

For a moment Ben stood in the cold not sure what to do next. The sight of his father carrying a steaming kettle startled him.

"I'm afraid your mother has caught a nasty cold, son. But there's no need for the two of us to be awake. Go back to bed. Aunt Hett and I can manage."

Ben nodded sleepily. "See you in the morning, then." With the sound of his mother's hacking cough behind him, he stumbled back into the attic toward his bed. He remembered past winters when his own chest had burned with the pain of coughs like his mother's. Many a night she had sat by him and kept a bowl of strong-smelling herbs steaming to help him breathe. That was probably what Aunt Hett was doing now.

Morning came at last, and still the anguished coughing continued to come from the sickroom. Ben dressed quickly while Zack, who was already up, waited.

Zack shook his head sympathetically. "Granny say that kind of coughing needs powerful medicine."

Abigail looked almost matronly in her apron and a cap that didn't quite hide her red hair as she spooned thick porridge into their bowls. The men had eaten, and Aunt Hett was still upstairs in the sickroom.

"I'm sorry about your ma," Abigail said politely. "We had to wait several minutes in the bitter cold for the omnibus after the program."

Ben had almost forgotten the show he and Zack had missed. As if she had read his mind, Abigail added, "By the way, The Spirit of the Alps, whatever it was, looked to me like mist in the mountains. Someone said it was all done with trick photography."

She was being extra kind this morning. What she did not say was that the whole thing had been the most thrilling, wonderful experience of her life. Furthermore, she planned to see for herself places like the Great Wall of China, the Palace of Thebes in Egypt, and certainly Yellowstone, Wyoming. Visions of the vast scenes from the show, which looked so real you could almost step into them, flashed in her mind. It was a while before the reality of where she was dawned on her. The food sitting before her was growing cold, and Ben and Zack were staring at her with a peculiar look on their faces. Had she said something? With a toss of her head and a scowl she slid quickly into her old self.

Aunt Hett stood in the doorway. Lines of tiredness creased her face. "Abigail, those bundles of clothes and the soup for the O'Briens need to be taken to the mission this morning. After that, you are on your own." She smiled at them all. "Coughs like these take their time and toll. The best thing you can do to help is to see to your own day. Mind, you are the hostess now, Abigail."

Weighed down with heavy bundles, the boys trudged along behind Abigail. "Some hostess," Ben grumbled. "She acts more like the Tsar of Russia." Abigail's idea to take the clothes and food directly to the family in the Five Points instead of to the mission, where it would sit until one of the missionaries could make the delivery, was just plain crazy. But nothing he or Zack said could persuade her differently. Her haughty offer to go alone had been the deciding factor. So here they were, heading for trouble. Ben could feel it in his bones.

The Five Points slum had not changed since Ben's last visit. Raggedly dressed children ran in its streets. Drunks stumbled past, and foulness was everywhere. Pigs rooting in the garbage made walking treacherous.

True to his instinctive feeling, things went wrong from the start. Mrs. O'Brien lay sick in her bed with the miseries. Her brood of children were all too young to help. Some of them could barely toddle around the stark room. They stared at the newcomers, especially Zack, in wondering silence. Mr. O'Brien was out hunting for work. The family, like so many in Five Points, were immigrants who had just recently come from Ireland and were badly in need of basic household goods.

Cold ashes lay in the small stove where a fire should have burned. The last of the coal had been burnt the night before and all of their small store of wood too. While Abigail fetched water from the courtyard, Ben and Zack purchased sticks and coal from an evil-looking old man who charged them most of Ben's pocket money.

It took Zack a long time to coax the fire to heat the soup. Together he and Ben fed the children as fast as they could. Meanwhile, Abigail took care of the mother. When the last child was fed and the clothes distributed they left.

Outside, somewhere in the city, the chimes of a church bell rang the noon hour. Thick dark clouds covering the sky threatened a snowstorm. As soon as they stepped into the street the wind gripped them. It whipped Ben's muffler across his face and forced Zack and Abigail to put their heads down. No one noticed the gang of small boys slipping like shadows from the doorways of adjacent tenements.

In a moment, Ben found himself face-to-face with a figure in a top hat, a ragged coat, and boots that were obviously too large for their owner. "And if it ain't the bleedin' charity boys doing their good deeds for the day," he said, blocking Ben's way.

Ben looked around quickly, only to see that both Zack and Abigail were ringed in by a menacing pack of equally ragged, top-hatted young boys. None of them could be as old as he and Zack. With his back against the tenement wall, he sized up the boy in front of him; then his heart sank. This was not to be a fair fight. In the boy's right hand a stout club of wood studded with bits of metal rose threateningly.

"We don't want your kind 'round here." The boy took a step closer to Ben. "So you just go on back to where you come from, see?" He raised the club higher. "And so's you remember what I'm telling you, I'm gonna teach you good." Laughter rose from the rest of the boys as their leader grabbed Ben's muffler.

A sudden shout broke the tension. "Fire, fire!" the voice yelled. "The whole blooming waterfront's going up. Pickin's for all. Fire, fire!" As the voice continued to shout, others joined in the cry.

The boy who had been about to smash Ben hesitated. Then he released Ben's muffler, commanded his gang to follow on the double, and ran in the direction of the waterfront.

Ben could hear his heart racing. Zack and Abigail hurried to his side. Everywhere people rushed past them toward the waterfront.

A low voice behind them made the three of them spin around. "Listen, unless you all want to be killed, don't just stand there. Run before they find out there ain't any fire." It was Letti. For a few seconds she stood like a mirage facing them. Before they could stop her she was off and running hard toward the supposed fire.

Abigail started to run after Letti. "No!" Ben grabbed his cousin by the arm and held her. "You heard Letti. If they come back and we're still here there's no telling what will happen. Let's go."

"Right," Zack said. "That Letti saved our skins this time. Same trick maybe won't work twice in one day." Between them they flanked Abigail and pulled her with them as they ran. When they were safely out of sight of Five Points and well into a good neighborhood, they walked. In spite of the running they had done, Abigail hugged her arms to keep warm. Her face was pale.

Gently, as if he were dealing with a frightened horse, Zack said, "'Pears to me like something more going on than a body can see. Now you take Letti.

She looked mighty good for somebody supposed to be living in the slum." It was true. Letti had looked neatly dressed and clean. "I 'spect she risked her neck hollering fire like that." He chuckled. "Smart like a fox, that one. Don't think I'd be worrying too much 'bout her, Miss Abigail."

Abigail raised her eyes to Zack's. "It's plain Abigail," was all she said. By the time they reached home the color had come back to her face. The whole thing had been her fault, her idea to take the bundles to Five Points instead of the mission. She would just have to bear the responsibility. On the other hand, if she hadn't disobeyed they might never have seen Letti. Or would they?

A black carriage pulled by a fat gray mare stood in front of the house. Its owner, accompanied by Ben's father, was just coming down the steps.

Ben reached the gate in time to hear his father say, "Thank you, doctor. I don't know what we'd have done without you."

The doctor nodded. "Complete rest, no visitors. See that she takes her medicine. The fever should be down by morning, and your wife will feel a whole lot better. I'll look in on her later today." He tipped his hat to Abigail as he passed to his carriage.

For the rest of the day, with hushed voices and silent footsteps, the household revolved around the sick patient. Uncle Hiram and Ben's father left briefly for a meeting. Aunt Hett spent most of her time upstairs with Ben's mother. The doctor came a second time and went, satisfied that his patient was doing well.

At supper Abigail, Ben, and Zack ate alone at the kitchen table. No one spoke about the morning's events. Aunt Hett had been too busy and distracted even to ask Abigail how things had gone at the mission.

While they ate, Abigail took a piece of folded paper from her apron pocket. Printed across it the name "Abigail" stood out in large bold letters. She spread the paper on the table in front of them and said, "I found this under the back door to the kitchen just before supper. Here, read it."

Ben turned the square of paper toward him and read, "I am sorry to cause trouble. There is no other way I can think of. Please don't try to find me. Stay out of Five Points unless you go with one of the missionaries or your mum. The Plug Uglies boys are a mean bunch. Your friend, Letti. P. S. I am sorry that someone is sick at your house and hope it is not your mum."

"Don't that beat all," Zack said, raising his eyebrows.

"What it means," Abigail stated, "is that Letti was here. How else could she know that someone was sick?"

"And if she came while the doctor was here, none of us would have seen her," Ben added. "All of us were in the parlor till he left."

Abigail nodded. "Right. Everybody knows the doctor's carriage. She must have seen it, crept 'round the back of the house, then added that last line."

"Whatever Letti's up to," Ben said, "it seems to me she's playing with fire running around in the Five Points." He hadn't meant a pun, but as Abigail and Zack broke out laughing it struck him. Letti had indeed played with fire that morning.

Out in the dark, Letti hurried down a narrow lane toward Marm's school. She would have given much even to be near a fire. The bitter wind whipped through her thin shawl. She could no longer feel her toes inside her shoes. As an icy tear ran down her cheek, fears filled her mind. Maybe it was Abigail's mum lying sick in bed. What if she had brought that on the only folks in this world who had ever really cared for her?

7

Caught in a Blizzard

Ben knew he should not go into the sickroom, but two days had passed since he had seen his mother. His father had already left for the mission, and Uncle Hiram had gone to work at the telegraph company. He could hear Aunt Hett and Susie in the nursery. Downstairs Zack was showing Abigail how to make corn pone. Carefully Ben inched open the door to his mother's room and moved quietly to the big curtained bed.

Her eyes were closed, and her face was pale against the white pillows. He hadn't meant to awaken her, only to see her for a moment. Still, he didn't move when she looked up at him.

"Ben," she whispered weakly. Her eyes lit slightly.

Ben grasped her hand in his and bent to kiss her cheek. It felt cool to him, but her hand in his was limp. "The doctor said you're going to be fine."

She smiled and turned her head away to cough. "Sorry," she whispered. "I am lots better, really."

Ben wasn't sure. Maybe he should not have disturbed her. He had never seen her this sick before. "You rest, now," he said and patted her hand. "I'm not supposed to be in here. Doctor's orders." He grinned sheepishly.

With a wink to let him know she understood, she smiled, pressed his hand, and closed her eyes. Ben left quickly before Aunt Hett came to check her patient.

Back in the kitchen, Abigail had turned out the corn pone. In spite of the fact that his recipe called for coon fat instead of fat back, Zack was attacking his third piece with relish. "Never would've knowed the difference," he said. He motioned to Ben to try some.

"That smells wonderful," Aunt Hett said as she came into the kitchen. "Ben, I've an errand for you and Zack, if you'd be so kind. I can't spare Abigail today with Susie so fussy and your ma needing all the rest she can get." She held out an envelope and a small purse. "In this cold you'll have to take the omnibus up Broadway to the corner of Liberty street and get off right in front of the Telegraph Company. I know your uncle meant to take this envelope with him this morning. You just go in and ask for him." Upstairs Susie had begun to wail. Aunt Hett frowned. "Land sakes, I don't know what's got into that child today," she said and rushed from the room.

Without a word Zack looked at Ben, and Ben knew what they both were thinking. It was all he could do to keep from whooping aloud in front of Abigail. Freedom at last!

From the moment they entered the telegraph company they were surrounded by the sound of clicking, like the drone of thousands of beetles on a hot July day. Most of the workers were women who barely glanced at Ben and Zack. A pleasant clerk took the envelope Ben handed him and returned shortly to usher them into his uncle's office.

"A bit impressive, lads, eh?" Uncle Hiram winked. "Those hundreds of clicks you hear are sending messages clear across the United States." He tapped one great hand against the desk top. "Now, if we were a little richer we'd have wires straight to the house, and I'd tap out a note to your aunt saying that you both arrived with the envelope. This," he said holding up the envelope, "is going to save me a lot of bother."

Ben grinned. "But so long as you don't have that wire, sir, Zack and me were planning to explore the city for a while before we go back."

"Why didn't I think of that?" Uncle Hiram said with a twinkle in his eye. "However, I don't relish what your aunt would say if I let you go wandering around the city in this cold." He opened a desk drawer and took out a handful of coins. "Suppose you two ride up Fifth Avenue and see what you can see, say as far as St. Patrick's Cathedral on 50th Street. The work on it has been stopped till this war is over, but you can look around, and it's a grand sight, that." He handed the coins to Ben. "Mind you don't go off on your own. The city is a big place."

Ben held up the small purse from Aunt Hett. "Thank you, sir, but we still have the fare home."

"So you do. Then I shall save half for another day." Ben returned the extra money, slipped the rest into the purse, and thanked his uncle once more.

The ride to St. Patrick's took longer than Ben expected. The fashionable homes they had seen along Fifth Avenue went as far north as 37th Street. By the time they reached the huge cathedral they were well away from the settled part of the city. In spite of the cold that stung and made them turn their backs to the slightest wind, they walked around the great unfinished church, awed by its massive stone skeleton and ghost-like silence. Perhaps because of the cold, no one else was around. Wooden slabs partially covered a section of wall where the foundation was exposed. Ben thought it must go down deeper than anything he had ever seen, but it was hard to tell how deep from where they stood outside the fence that protected the site.

Zack, with his muffler pulled up across his mouth, pointed toward the gathering of thick gray clouds overhead. "We sure in for snow," he said.

Ben nodded. "Better catch the next omnibus."

Once or twice a lone carriage passed by quickly as they waited. Large flakes of snow were already falling. Across the street the omnibus going north appeared and stopped in front of the cathedral to let off a heavily bundled workman, probably the watchman.

Just then a fine carriage pulled by a team of black horses passed between them and the bus. For one fleeting moment Ben saw the young woman's face pressed against the window—Letti's. Zack had seen her too. "Letti!" he said in amazement.

Almost instantly the horses passed, and she was gone.

"Come on," Ben said. "We can follow her in the bus." Waving his arms and running madly he raced to the omnibus with Zack behind him. The driver waited for them impatiently with a gruff command to hurry it up.

Ben paid their fare. The six-cent fare would take them as far as they liked. Zack chose a window seat for them in the nearly empty bus. In the distance the carriage bearing Letti hurried down the street. If only they could see where she got off they might be able to get an address or something that would help locate her. The excitement of the chase gripped Ben till he forgot everything else.

Loosening his muffler, Zack said admiringly, "Mighty fine pair of horses pulling that carriage. What you reckon that girl got herself into now?"

Ben continued to keep his eyes on the object of their hunt. "Could be any of a dozen reasons," he said. "Maybe she got herself adopted." He didn't really think so, not in the short time since they had seen her last. "More likely, she stole it somewhere, or some of her friends did."

For several moments the tenseness of following Letti held them. Though in reality they had already traveled for fifteen minutes, it seemed less to Ben. When the carriage ahead of them turned to the left, Ben called out quickly to be let off.

The driver slowed to a halt, grumbling angrily about boys who didn't know their own minds, and pulled away almost the instant Zack and Ben climbed down.

Luckily, Letti's carriage was still in sight. But as Ben stared at it through the snow, it turned left once more.

Zack hunched his shoulders against the cold. "Nothing we can do to catch her now. The only thing we better catch is the next ride home."

While Ben stood debating with himself, the wind rose and drove the snow in blinding circles in front of them. Something inside him sounded a warning. "Right," he said. "At least we know where to look for her. And I'd recognize that carriage anywhere." He comforted himself with the thought that it hadn't been for nothing after all.

The snow started to cover the road in earnest. "Might as well try to see through a cloud of feathers," he shouted above the wind. Only a few feet away from where they stood waiting, whirling snow blotted out the rest of the world. Ben shoved his hands inside his empty pockets for extra warmth. Empty! He had given the last of his change to the bus driver.

Zack's money lay safely in his bag back in the attic. "I say we walk back till we see a bus and hail it," he said, wiping snow from his face. "Most folks be willing to help a body out in a storm like this." Zack drew his muffler up till only his eyes showed.

Ben nodded and did the same. "Freeze to death

if we stay here," he muttered. The wind was behind them, but he could see no more than three feet ahead of them.

After a few moments Zack knelt and brushed the snow away from in front of him. "Cobblestones," he said. "If we stick to the street we can follow it back." They could walk with the cobblestones underfoot as a guide. But soon all sense of direction vanished as they plowed on through the blinding snow that covered even the rough stones. More and more often they halted to dig for signs of the road. At the last stop, the thing they feared happened.

Zack's fingers were numb with cold. He stopped his searching and stood up. Ben still crouched down digging, and Zack shook him by the shoulder. "It's no use. No way we can tell where that road is, and nothing gonna be traveling on it anyway in this." For what seemed like hours they had walked without seeing a single carriage or omnibus.

Ben stood up. "They've stopped running in this blizzard. There has to be a house somewhere around here or something." His voice sounded strangely thin to him. Maybe they should stop walking for a while and rest a little.

Zack shook Ben's arm. "We got to keep moving so's we find that warm fire waiting for us." Stumbling, he pulled Ben along.

"You think your pa gonna let us just stay out here? He and your uncle probably be lookin' for us right now. Got to listen for the horses coming."

Ben thought of his father and strained to hear the

sound of galloping horses as they walked with shoulders hunched against the wind. He could almost smell the smoke of the imagined fire. The biting wind rushed behind them like a freezing hand that clutched his back. He glanced at Zack, whose face and muffler were caked with ice, and felt the same stiffness on his own. It was his fault they were here at all. Headlines from yesterday's newspaper flashed across his mind: "Soldier Frozen to Death at Fort Pillow." If they didn't find shelter soon they could freeze to death. By chasing Letti he had, without thinking, plunged them both into danger. Now what?

From deep inside him his father's repeated words welled up: "Pray, son. Nothing is too hard for the Lord or too small to bring to him." Being lost in a blizzard was no small thing. "Lord Jesus," he prayed, "we're lost, and we need help, and it's my fault." He remembered Uncle Hiram's prayer for Letti. "Please find your strayed sheep," he added.

Without warning, his foot struck something so hard it shot pain through his numbed toes. He groaned and bent to examine the damage. Barely visible beneath its snow cover lay a discarded fence post. A little ahead and to his right lay another. Ben lifted his head as the faint odor of smoke came to him.

"It's fire, Zack! Do you smell it?" he cried.

Zack cupped his mittened hands close to his nose. "I smell it," he yelled. Zigzagging first left, then right, they tried to follow the odor of smoke, sometimes losing it in the wall of snow, then find-ing it again.

Suddenly Zack saw something directly in front of them. "It's a fence," he said. As they clung to the wooden posts they followed the fence to where it rounded a corner away from the worst of the wind. Ahead of them, barely visible, was a section of stone footing. "It's the cathedral," Zack shouted.

"Down there," Ben pointed. "I see a light down there."

The smell of burning wood was heavy. Someone had a fire going inside the pit below the church. Light showed through the cracks in the boarded section of wall. With renewed strength the two made their way over the fence and knelt to peer between the boards.

They could see little else beyond the fire blazing away below. Together they pounded on the walls and shouted to whoever was down there to help them.

8

A Strange Angel

When they listened for an answer, Ben heard nothing. Zack shook his head. Whoever was down there did not hear them. "There has to be a way inside," Ben said. He began to pull at the tightly nailed boards.

Zack felt the boards in front of him. His hands groped for a loose plank. "Must be one somewhere." Together they made their way along the base of the wall. At the far corner the lowest board moved slightly as they touched it. Tearing at it eagerly, they found it lifted easily to expose the very entrance they sought.

They could see the fire below plainly now. In its light they saw that the drop to the bottom of the pit was too far for them to descend without a ladder. Ben leaned as far into the hole as he dared to look for a way down. Someone had cleverly attached a thick rope to the next wooden plank. With both hands he pulled until the full length lay at their feet. It was long and heavy.

"Looks like this is how whoever's down there got in," Ben said.

"You reckon we can get down with this too?"

Zack asked, examining the hardened, worn section in his hand.

"We have no choice," Ben answered. "If we stay out here in this blizzard we don't stand a chance. I'm going down. You steady the rope and follow when I give the signal."

Ben gripped the rope, closed his eyes, and pushed himself through the hole. For a moment he swung in the empty air, then slowed as above him Zack tried to hold the rope still against the wall.

With the same coaxing tone of voice Zack used to calm a frightened horse he now coached Ben. "Steady you go, easy now, don't fret. You just doin' fine."

Ben's wet mittens slid on the rope, making him lock his feet together to slow himself. With a thud he was down on the hard ground below. Zack followed quickly.

"Hello, anybody here?" Ben called. An eerie silence enveloped the great stone walls. Nothing stirred except the crackling flames of the fire ahead. In its light they could see that they were in some sort of storage room. Scaffolding, ropes, canvas, huge half-carved statues, and various other things lay scattered about in enormous heaps. Cautiously Ben approached the fire. "Hello," he called again. "Is anybody down here?"

It was clear that someone had been. Zack picked up a long stick lying near the fire and moved a half-burned fence post nearer to the flames. "Never know any fire built itself so good. This one singing like a bird." Zack spread his wet coat and muffler over two sticks stuck in the ground close to the heat. "'Pears like somebody knows just how to do down here."

Ben pulled off his own wet things and threw them over a large stone close enough to feel warm to his touch. His feet were nearly frozen, and his whole body shook as he crouched by the heat. Zack held his hands almost in the flames.

Ben toasted first his back then the front of him, and little by little his body warmed. "Zack, when we were almost goners outside, I could hear my pa's voice saying, 'Pray, son.' And here's this fire and nobody around. You think maybe this ain't no ordinary fire?"

Zack raised his head. His black face glistened with sweat. "It sure beats all. You thinkin' the Lord's angel made this here fire? I know one thing for sure: Without it we'd be frozen 'fore we find our way in this storm."

Out of a canvas-covered heap a little way from the fire came a voice that startled Ben and nearly tumbled Zack into the flames. "Been called a pile of things, but never no angel before this." The owner of the voice appeared from under the canvas. He was a boy near their own age. For a minute his thin white face turned wary as Ben stood to his feet.

"Why didn't you answer when we hollered?" Ben asked. Without waiting for a reply from the boy, he added, "All we want is shelter from the blizzard outside, then we'll be on our way."

Gently Zack said, "Old Grandpa Bell always say, 'The Lord do his work in mysterious ways. He sure did use your fire, or we still be out there. Couldn't see three feet ahead of us. The smell of wood burning led us right here." Zack stopped to chuckle. "Pretty near had us thinking you was an angel."

At that the boy relaxed his tightly clenched fists and came jauntily over to sit by the fire. "Have to wait till the watchman makes his rounds the times I come here. Regular as clockwork he is and old too. Never looks in here, just walks round the building, tries the locks, and heads on home."

"That must have been the old man we saw get off the omnibus in front of the cathedral," Ben said. Bit by bit he told the boy the details of how they had made their way to his hideout.

"Name's Colin," he said, extending a grimy hand first to Ben, then to Zack. "I knowed a fellow lost his way in a storm like this one. Turned up frozen solid as a block of ice. Found him twenty yards from the railroad station. Trains wasn't running. Guess he never saw the depot." Colin had brought out a bag of hard rolls, two brown, wrinkled apples, a shriveled carrot, and a tin pot of water. He divided them equally among the three of them.

"Mighty handy, that rope," Colin remarked as he filled a mug with hot water for Ben. "I can lower most anything by it before I slide down here myself."

Ben nodded. They hadn't eaten since breakfast,

and even the stale bread tasted good. Ben let the hot water warm his mouth before he swallowed, then passed the mug back to Colin.

Twice Colin dragged wood for the fire from under his canvas storage. Outside, the wind still raged. Snow sifted between the spaces in the planked wall above them, covering places on the floor a few feet from where they sat. Ben could feel the cold at his back and edged nearer to the fire. After a while, Colin produced canvas covers and piles of newspapers to use for beds and blankets. The three of them huddled in their makeshift tents as close to the warmth as they dared. Colin looked almost content to Ben in spite of their bare surroundings.

"How'd you come to be here, Colin?" he asked.

He thought a moment before he answered. "Weren't no choice but to leave," he said. "After Ma died, my pa took to beating me terrible. Didn't make no difference what for. Pa never knowed. Just drank himself near to death. Didn't care about nothing else." Colin poked the fire and cleared his throat. "When Ma was alive, she used to talk about the good old days 'fore we come to Cow Bay. Back then Pa worked steady, and Ma took in sewing. We was living real comfortable like. Then one day Pa lost his job and after that couldn't seem to find no piece of luck. Things went on down the chute till we ended up living in Cow Bay. Guess Ma might still be alive if Pa hadn't started his drinking." Colin poked the fire once more and sat back, lost in thought.

"Where's Cow Bay?" Ben asked.

"Ain't nowhere now, since the city took it down," Colin said. "Used to be just like Five Points, no place a body'd want to be."

Ben reported their own encounter with the Five Points, including Letti's part in their rescue. Zack added his impressions, interrupted now and then by Colin's hearty laugh and his "Been there myself, a time or two."

Colin hugged his knees and looked serious. "You boys watch out now down around the Five Points. Them in the top hats is the Plug Uglies gang. And don't go walking early or late by the waterfront either. Daybreak boys'll catch you sure. Nights it's the River Rats."

Ben broke in, "River Rats was Letti's old gang."

"Bad ones," Colin said. "Steal from their own mothers if they could, and as soon murder you as look at you if you get in their way."

After a while Ben asked, "What will you do now, Colin?"

"I 'spect I'll be heading west one of these days. Hear there's plenty of work if you're willing. You go to school?" he asked Ben suddenly.

"Soon's we get back to Tarrytown I'll be going again, I guess," Ben replied. "Zack, too."

Colin looked at Zack with new respect in his eyes. "Went when we first came to the city. Always thought I'd like to go back one day. Pa wouldn't let me. Anyways, you got to have proper clothes for school." He laughed heartily.

Sitting up straight, Ben stared at Colin. "What

about the mission? They'd take you in, give you a place to sleep, and send you to school right there."

"Send me straight out to be an indentured apprentice soon's they could, too. The law says an orphan can be hired out till he's twenty-one to learn a trade. Half the time their masters don't feed indentured apprentices barely enough to keep 'em alive. And there's nothing a fellow can do about it. Unless he's lucky enough to run away without being caught and beaten sore."

"But couldn't you go to the police and tell them if you're not treated fairly?" Ben asked.

Colin looked at Ben. "There's a lot you don't know about the city," he said. "First off, Boss Tweed's got the city government in his pocket, including who gets the inspectors' jobs, the police chief's, the mayor's, the street cleaners', everyone. Anybody who can make a dishonest nickel off the city is a man after the Boss's heart." Colin whistled and stirred up the fire to a hot blaze.

"And suppose you did find an honest policeman, he's bound by the law to send you right back. Now, if you're a vagrant and under legal age, you could be sent to the almshouse. That's supposed to be a place to take care of the poor." Colin whistled again. "Starve you there too. Put you in with all the old people, mad ones and all. Soon's you're old enough out you go to be indentured and learn a trade. Rather die than go there." He poked the fire once more. "Besides, being free there's odd jobs to pick up, and I don't need for much more than this."

Zack said quietly, "Guess I know what you mean. Almshouse ain't no better nowhere."

Colin nodded and looked at Ben. "What are you two planning to do come morning? Won't be anything moving in the city much tomorrow till the roads are cleared some."

"Guess we'll have to walk home," Ben said. "At least by morning maybe we can see where we're going."

Colin excused himself and disappeared behind one of the heaps in a far corner of the room. When he returned Ben did the same, and Zack too. For protection during the night Colin showed them how to ring the fire with large chunks of stone so that no one would accidentally roll into the hot coals. Between them they built up the fire and stocked a good supply of wood close at hand.

Outside, the storm howled on. Its cold breath reached through the canvas wrapped around Ben. He curled himself up under his newspapers so that only a small opening remained for his eyes and stared at the fire. In its shadows the piles of scaffolding, unfinished marble statues, and heaps of refuse looked like giant figures silently watching. Watchers like guardian angels, Ben thought sleepily. Who would have thought he and Zack would end up sleeping in St. Patrick's Cathedral? Ben smiled as his eyes close. He was sure that God was smiling too.

9

Discovery

Ben awakened shivering and wondered at first where he was. Morning had come with overcast skies. The wind no longer howled, but snow still sifted down through the cracks between the boards. Even now his father and Uncle Hiram could be out looking for them. His mother must be frantic. He remembered her pale, worn face and pushed the canvas blanket aside. Zack looked out sleepily from his own wrappings.

Colin was already up and busy. "One thing a fellow learns," he said. "You want to leave things the way you found them."

Together the three of them worked to erase all traces of the fire. They carried the stones back to their old heap and stored away the extra canvases. When they were ready to go, Ben looked up at the rope he had slid down the previous night. The distance to the top seemed greater than before.

With his pack tied to his waist, Colin pulled on a pair of ragged-topped boots big enough to fit over his own thin shoes. Though the soles of the boots were nearly worn through, each of the heels had a large nail sticking out. "You grip the rope, dig in

your heels, and up you go step by step," he
explained. "That rope can take all the digging you
give it." The old rope, though frayed, was as thick
as Ben's wrist.

Colin climbed first. At the top he disappeared
through the gap in the wooden plank. Moments
later down came the boots. Then it was Zack's turn.
He made it up without accident, then threw the
boots to Ben.

Ben laced the tops tightly around his legs, grabbed
the rope, and climbed. Twice a boot caught in the
rope and refused to budge till Ben pried it free. At
the top at last, he crawled through into knee-deep
snow.

It was still snowing lightly. Last night's wind had
blown some parts of the road almost clean and piled
great drifts across it in other places. From where
the three of them stood the whole world seemed
covered with white. Nothing stirred in the silence
except the light swish of falling snow. Colin
replaced the wooden plank so that it looked like
the others; then single file they walked toward the
fence.

Not a carriage or a horse was anywhere. Zack
hunched his shoulders and let out a low whistle.
"Don't remember this much snow ever. Nobody out
here today but us."

"You can bet on that," Colin said. "What are you
fellows planning to do?"

Until now it hadn't occurred to Ben that they
needed a plan. With everything shut down by the

storm, they were back on foot once more. In all this snow it would take hours to get home.

As if he read Ben's thoughts, Zack looked at him. "Folks living somewhere around here might be willing to help out till we can get on our way again."

Pointing with his free hand toward the northeast, Colin offered to take them with him. "I'm aiming for better pickings over that way. There's a few cottages on the other side of the hill. One of 'em belongs to a widow lady, and sometimes for an odd job she's needing done, I make out middling fair."

Ben pointed in the general direction Letti's carriage had taken when it left the main road. "Any idea what's over that way?" he asked Colin.

Colin laughed. "Best garbage in the city," he said. "Only one or two places out there, big houses with rich folk. Trouble is it's real hard to get close to rich houses what with the gardeners and servants around. Be a heap easier where I'm heading."

Ben felt his throat tighten. Had last night's food been somebody's garbage? He would never again complain about the food set before him. Should they go with Colin or try the big houses?

He looked at Zack hoping for an answer, then back at Colin.

Colin watched Ben's face closely. "Over there's where your Letti's carriage went, ain't it? I suppose you'll be wanting to find out what you can."

Ben nodded.

"You fellows watch out for yourselves," Colin

said and gave a final pat to the bulging pockets of his tattered coat. "Maybe one of these days our tracks will cross. Never know when you might need another angel." He laughed, hefted his pack, and began to walk through the deep snow toward the hill that led to the widow's place.

For a few seconds Ben stood with Zack and watched the jaunty figure of Colin. Then with a sigh Ben put his mind to the hike ahead of them.

Zack chuckled. "You reckon we'll run into that Colin again? Talk about being free, guess he knows more about that than most folks."

The idea of eating garbage made Ben wonder. How many days did Colin really go hungry? Anyone could see that he was far too thin, even though his clothes were sizes too big for him. And what would happen if he did get caught one of those days? The almshouse, or worse, the Tombs? At least for that day Colin was free.

The snow stretched endlessly, but they had a goal now. Someone in the big houses would certainly help them once they told their story. This was the way Letti's carriage had gone, Ben thought. If they were lucky, they might even spot it again. An hour later they passed the first hedges of a long drive leading to one of the fashionable houses.

At almost the same moment a large black horse came stumbling through the snow along the drive. It floundered in the deeper drifts directly ahead of Ben and Zack. In an instant Zack plowed his way into the drifts toward the horse.

"Be careful, Zack," Ben cried out. The horse reared up snorting as Zack approached. Zack slowed his pace as he moved closer, talking in a low gentle voice. Once more the horse reared. Its eyes were wild. Zack stayed motionless. "Easy, boy, easy," he said. "That's it, stand a while till we both catches our breath." Slowly Zack reached out his hand and patted the horse's trembling sides. By the time Ben reached them, Zack had hold of the horse's mane. Gently he backed him out of the drift.

From the direction of the house a gentleman came limping down the drive. As he approached, Ben saw that the man's face looked drawn and pale. Someone else was coming too. From his clothes Ben guessed that the old man hurrying toward them was either the gardener or the stable keeper. Most likely he was the stable keeper for he had an anxious look on his face as he slipped a lead rope around the horse's neck.

"Ah, he's a bad one, Captain. Pushed open the door and bolted he did," the old man said.

"So it seems, George. Take him on up, and see to it that his stall is well secured." At the gentleman's order the keeper nodded and led the horse away.

For a moment Ben thought he saw a frown on the young man's face while he watched the older man make his way back to the stables. The look passed as he turned questioning eyes on Ben and Zack. "Well, sirs, just what are you doing here?"

"We were hoping to find someone around here,"

Ben began. Briefly he explained how they had visited St. Patrick's Cathedral, had been stranded in the storm, and had spent the night in the church. He made no mention of Colin or Letti.

The man looked hard at Ben, then at Zack. "Are you telling me you two survived last night's blizzard on your own?"

Zack nodded. "Couldn't have done it without a good fire and something to keep out the wind," he said.

"There was plenty of wood, old fence posts, and scrap left by the workmen," Ben added. "Even some canvases."

The man smiled and laid a hand on each boy's shoulders. "Well done, lads. I expect you could do with a hot meal. Come, and we'll see what Martha can find for you." He started toward the house chuckling to himself. His firm grip moved Ben and Zack with him. "Tell me what brought two lads like yourself to visit St. Patrick's in January?"

Ben explained about his father's church in Tarrytown, the visit to his uncle's, and the meeting at Cooper Union, everything except the part about Letti. Several times the man asked questions. Ben worried that he had said more than he ought.

The house at the end of the driveway was elegant, a mansion in the gracious style of a southern plantation home. Ben raised his eyebrows as he glanced at Zack. Beside the tall white pillars of the veranda, wide second-story windows opened onto balconies.

While they stood gazing at the splendid house the gentleman said, "Puzzling isn't it, lads, why my father chose to build away out here. At any rate, my southern grandmother would have been pleased with the style. He raised one hand in mock salute to the house. "I am the sole occupant and the last surviving member of the Sikes family. I doubt Grandmother would have approved of her grandson, a captain in the Union army, but I daresay my father would have been pleased had he lived to see the day."

Leaning heavily on Zack and Ben once more, he led them up the stone steps to the massive wooden door. He was breathing hard by the time they reached the top step. "Wounded in the leg fighting down in Tennessee—haven't got my strength back," the captain explained. He opened the door and ushered Ben and Zack inside.

Ben looked at the captain with new respect, then drew in his breath at the sight before him. Life-size marble statues stood on pedestals at either side of a grand staircase that curved to the top floor. Enormous paintings hung on the dark polished walls. Several doors with gleaming brass knobs lined the entry hall.

An old woman with a round cheerful face framed by a white cap came through a wide archway to their left. "Tch, Captain, you oughtn't be running out after that devil of a horse. You will be catching the fever again," she fussed. "My George will look after him now."

"Yes, indeed, he will," the captain replied. "Meanwhile, Martha, do you suppose you could fix up these lads with something to eat? I believe they haven't eaten since yesterday noon."

"Land sakes!" the old woman exclaimed. She peered at Ben and Zack as if she expected to see signs of starvation. "You boys come right on into my kitchen, and we'll have you warmed and fed soon as a body can stir the pot." She led the way through the open door past another hallway of dark wood doors, turned left and then right once again.

On the kitchen hearth an iron pot of something gave off an aroma that set Ben's mouth to watering. True to her word the old woman ladled out two full bowls of thick soup and set them before Ben and Zack at the large kitchen table. While they ate she fetched soft white bread, slabs of cheese, apple cake, and steaming mugs of cider.

At last Ben felt utterly stuffed. Zack, too, was full. He set his empty mug down and said softly, "Can't remember somethin' tastin' this good."

The captain reappeared. He patted the old woman's arm affectionately. "There's nothing like Martha's cooking to set a fellow feeling right. Now, Martha, it looks like we'll just have to keep our guests till this snow is off. Perhaps we can see them home safely tomorrow morning."

Ben's heart sank. What would another day's delay mean for his mother? She was probably frantic not knowing if he and Zack were dead or alive.

As if he had read Ben's thoughts, the captain reassured him with surprising news. "I've sent a telegraph message over the wire to be delivered to your parents at your uncle's home, telling them all is well and to expect you both safe and sound in the morning."

Zack grinned. "Don't that beat all," he said.

Ben felt a weight lift from him. There was nothing to worry about.

"We're a small crew here, lads. When I'm not home George and Martha keep things running smoothly."

"Used to be Mr. and Mrs. Grimes, the butler and his wife here with us before his old mother took sick. They went back to the old country," Martha said. "Of course, we've the new girl. Right smart she is and a big help with the linens and such."

"I'll have her make up beds in the lower east wing for the lads," the captain said, pulling a bell pull to signal for the maid. "While I take an afternoon rest—doctor's orders—you boys might want to give George a hand in the stable. I'm certain he'll find something of interest for you."

"Yes, sir," Ben said, and then forgot entirely what he meant to add. There in the doorway just behind the captain's back stood Letti. Her eyes were wide with shock.

Quickly she shook her head and pressed a finger to her lips. She curtsied as the captain turned to face her. "You rang, sir?"

"Yes, Lizzie," the captain said. "We have two young guests who'll be staying the night in the lower east wing. I'm sure they'd be comfortable in the blue room if you'll see to it."

"Right away, sir," Letti replied. She was gone in a flash.

10

The Promise

For the rest of the afternoon Ben and Zack helped George in the stables. When George left to fetch a forgotten tool, Ben hurried into the stall where Zack was pitching hay.

"We've got to talk," Ben said quickly. "What is that Letti up to calling herself Lizzie and pretending she didn't know us? She sure didn't want us to let on to the captain that we recognized her. I can't figure what she is doing working for the captain."

Zack looked serious. "She's up to somethin'. I've got a feeling it ain't right whatever it is."

Ben leaned on his shovel. "The trouble is, what do we do now? We can't just go back in there and tell the captain he's hired a thief. Besides, we don't have any proof."

"We didn't exactly tell Captain Sikes everything in the first place," Zack said. "Didn't mention chasing Letti and that carriage when the storm started. Reckon we better think on it before we get in any deeper."

They saw no more of Letti. As soon as supper was over Captain Sikes requested their company. The captain seemed interested in Ben and Zack's adventures, and Ben almost forgot about Letti. It was late when the boys finally were allowed to retire.

Martha led them to their room and bid them a cheery goodnight. The room held one enormous bed, a chest, a wardrobe, and a desk. Someone had banked the fire in the fireplace and placed warming pans between the bed sheets. "Letti, " Ben said, turning to Zack. "She must have been in here and fixed the room."

"Reckon so," Zack agreed. "Maybe she left a note somewhere." But there was no note, and reluctantly they gave up the search. It had been a long day. The bed with its deep feather pillows and blankets was softer than they could have imagined.

Lazily Ben yawned, then stopped abruptly at the sound of a soft knock on the door.

"It's me, Letti. Let me in."

Quickly Ben opened the door.

Shading a small candle in her hand, Letti brushed past him to set it on the dresser. She ignored Zack, who sat on the edge of the bed.

Ben closed the door behind her and turned to face her. "Okay, Letti or Lizzie, what's this all about?" he demanded.

Letti stood defiantly, her small chin raised, her eyes flashing. She had taken off her cap and let her thick, straw-colored hair hang about her shoulders so that she looked different from the plain serving girl she had seemed. "Well, you didn't give me away to the captain, and I guess I owe you for that. Though if your memory ain't too short, I saved your

skin back in Five Points, and that makes us even."
She crossed her arms with an air of superiority.

"Now suppose you tell me what you're doing
here. Sightseeing, Martha says, till you got lost in
the storm." Letti raised her chin higher. "Don't you
give me none of that. I know you followed me."

Ben felt his face grow hot. A wave of confusion
swept over him. Helplessly he looked at Zack, then
at Letti. "We, that is, Abigail, and, well, everybody
wondered what happened to you," he said. "You
didn't tell anybody you were going. Then we saw
you in front of Lord and Taylor's store."

Now Letti's face was red. "Didn't Abigail get my
note?" she asked.

"Well, yes," Ben stammered. "Sure, she got it,
but all you said was you had to take care of things.
We saw you in the carriage yesterday. We followed
till the carriage turned off from the main road, but
honestly, we didn't know till this morning you
were working here for Captain Sikes."

Zack, who had been quiet all this while, said,
"Miss Abigail sure been missin' you. I reckon the
whole family's feeling bad worrying about you,
Miss Letti. You reckon we could help you, Miss
Letti?"

Letti's lips trembled, and she clamped the lower
one with her teeth. With the back of her hand she
wiped her eyes. "If I level with you, both of you got
to promise not to tell anyone. That means no one
in the family, not the police, nobody from the mis-

sion, and no strangers. And that includes anybody in this household," she added.

Letti had pretty much covered everybody, Ben thought, but he wanted desperately to know what Letti was up to. He heard himself say, "Okay." Zack did the same.

Letti sat on the low chest. She pointed for Ben to join Zack on the bed. "You know that Plug Ugly gang you ran into back in the Five Points?" Ben nodded. "My brother is about that age. When our pa died we managed until our ma died of the fever. After that we were on our own like a lot of kids in the Five Points and the Bowery. As soon as I could, I joined up with the River Rats gang." Letti stopped and looked thoughtful for a moment. "That was before the mission and your Aunt Hett," she said.

"After the mission helped me find work at your aunt's, I tried to get Nat, my brother, to let them help him. But living on the streets makes a body powerful independent. Nat didn't want anything to do with the mission. The day I left your aunt's house I found a note from my old gang saying they had Nat, and if I wanted to see him alive again, I'd better come back where I belonged."

"But what are you doing here then?" Ben asked, puzzled.

"I figured I'd be a sitting duck to walk right into the gang's lap," Letti explained. "They don't take kindly to deserters. The only way I could think of was Marm's."

"Who is Marm?" Ben asked.

"Marm is what you might call the biggest head of crime in the city outside Boss Tweed's bunch, and even he won't mess with her operation. Like all the others, the River Rats are afraid of getting on the wrong side of Marm."

Zack interrupted. "You mean what this Marm says goes, and nobody dares to cross her?"

"Right," Letti replied. "So I figured if I joined up with Marm's street thieves, that would give me time to find out where Nat is and figure a way to get him out."

"So you were working for Marm the day we saw you and the boy take the woman's packages and purse."

Letti flushed red. "You nearly cost me my head chasing us like you did. The boy spilled the whole thing to Marm herself. The next thing I knew Marm had me pulled off the streets and enrolled in her school for servants."

"But what's this Marm doing running a school for servants?" Ben asked.

"It ain't what you think," Letti said. "The whole thing is to train a girl, give her false references, then once she's inside a rich house she spies out the place for Marm."

Ben felt his jaw slacken. "Is that what you're doing here?"

Looking away from him, Letti answered in a faltering voice. "I know it ain't right, but so far Marm has let me alone. For now, all I have to do is act like a serving girl should and keep my eyes and ears open."

"How is robbing the captain going to help your brother? Why not just go to the police?" Ben urged.

Letti looked at him with the wisdom of the streets in her eyes. "It ain't like that here, Ben. Marm's got it fixed so there's never proof that would stand up in a court if anybody dared cross her. As for the police, guess I already know more places to look for Nat than they do. I expect the word is already out to the gang that I'm working for Marm now. With me on the inside, it's a matter of time till the gang figures out something they want from me in exchange for Nat. That is, if I don't find him first."

"You mean some kind of information they could use to steal something before Marm's people find out about it?" Ben asked.

"Something like that, I guess," Letti said dejectedly. "I pray it don't come to that," she added. "If I could find out where Nat is and get to him, we could be on our way. All I'm asking you for is time."

Zack asked, "If you're here, Miss Letti, how're you gonna be looking for your brother?"

Letti answered him quickly. "Soon as the roads are clear, old George will drive me downtown to do the shopping for Martha. That gives me a couple of hours before George picks me up again. And once a week I'm to have the day off. George will take me to the omnibus stop in the morning, then pick me up there in the evening." She seemed confident.

"Okay," Ben said. "But what if Marm's man shows up with orders to rob the captain?"

Letti swallowed hard. "I'll make up an excuse. I don't know what yet. I won't let them hurt the captain."

Ben lowered his eyes. The candlelight glowed brightly but did little to chase the shadows he saw outside its small circle of light.

"Nat's my brother, and I've got to help him," Letti pleaded. "He ain't got nobody else."

A wave of pity swept over Ben. "There must be something we can do."

Taking the candle up, Letti stood. "You gave your word to keep mum. That's all I'm asking." With one hand on the door handle she added quietly, "Your pa's a preacher, ain't he?" Ben nodded. "Then maybe you could pray for Nat and me." She was gone before Ben could answer.

"Beats all," Zack said. "You reckon it's no accident, us turning up here right in the same house with Letti? Sort of like Colin and his fire being there when we needed it."

Ben stretched wearily. "Just the same, I don't see how we can help Letti and her brother out of this. What if Marm does send her thugs, and the captain gets hurt? I don't know, Zack, maybe we've got to tell this time."

Zack was already on his side of the bed under the heavy comforter. "How you gonna go back on your word, Ben?"

Miserable and cold, Ben climbed into his share of the bed. "Guess I need to think on it."

There was something in the back of his mind that he couldn't quite remember. What was it his pa had said last summer about loyalty? If he and Zack kept silent, maybe Letti would find Nat and the two of them get away. Then again, maybe there wouldn't be time. He pictured the captain's pale face and thin body. Captain Sikes and the two old people, George and Martha, would never be able to defend this large house without help. What was the right thing for him and Zack to do?

With his eyes tightly closed, Ben prayed. "It sure looks like a mess to me, Lord. I don't know if we should tell or not. Please take care of the captain and all of us tonight."

He must have fallen asleep then, because the next thing he knew the window rattled as if pebbles were hitting the glass. The bedside candle they had forgotten to blow out had burned until only a small stub remained, but it burned still. Holding it close, Ben stumbled to the window. The drapes were not quite closed, and with a shock Ben saw the thin face of Colin outside the window.

Awake too, Zack sat up. "What's Colin doin' out there?" he whispered.

As Ben opened the window, Colin grinned at him. "Lucky for me you fellows was on the ground floor. Saw your light and you sleeping like babies. Thought I'd pop in." He climbed through the window and stood gazing at the room. "Mighty grand, ain't it? What're you two doing here?"

"You aren't going to believe it, Colin," Ben said. "First Letti and now you." Quickly he filled Colin in on their finding the house and the captain's hospitality. Since Letti hadn't known about Colin she hadn't included him in her list of those he promised not to tell. For a second Ben hesitated, then told him everything about Letti and Nat, Marm, and the gang.

"Sounds bad," Colin said shaking his head. "Them River Rats are bad ones."

"Marm, too, from what we hear," Zack added.

Ben had almost forgotten his surprise at seeing Colin. Suddenly he remembered. "What in the world are you doing here?" he asked.

Colin scratched his head. "Tried the widow's place, but seems like she wasn't home. I figure she might have been visiting somewhere. Maybe stayed on because of the storm. Anyways, the place was locked up tight. I managed a bit of luck with the fruit cellar. Then I got to wondering about you fellows. This being the first house out this way I thought I'd take a look. Saw your light and here I am."

"You might as well bunk with us for the rest of the night," Ben said. This time he snuffed out the candle.

The sun was up long before the three awoke. At the light rap on the door Colin stiffened.

"It's me, Letti." Without waiting for an invitation she opened the door and entered.

Colin stared and Letti stared back. "I know you," he said. "You and your brother used to camp out down near the old theater."

Solemnly Letti looked at Colin. "We wondered what became of you," she said. "How'd you get in here?"

Colin explained. "I'll just be going soon's I get my stuff together, same way I came, through the window," he said.

From her pocket Letti produced a roll. "Here, take it and go quickly before the captain comes down for his breakfast." She handed the roll to Colin, who stuffed it into his shirt. "Mind you don't lift nothing of the captain's," she commanded. "And you two are to come down to the kitchen for breakfast."

When she had gone, Colin surveyed the room once more, his eyes lingering on the bed. "Best diggings I been in," he said. Ben wondered if he had ever slept in a real bed.

Zack helped lift the window, and together they watched as Colin disappeared around the side of the house.

"Got to admire his spunk, popping in here like he did last night," Zack said.

"Guess so," Ben said. "I wonder where he'll spend tonight." He didn't say it to Zack, but it seemed unfair that Colin had no real home, no mother, no family.

Before noon Ben's father and Uncle Hiram rode up to the captain's house on hired horses to fetch the boys. Clasped in his father's long arms Ben felt an overwhelming sense of relief and love all mixed together.

"Mom—is she okay?" In his heart Ben feared the answer.

"She'll be up within the week; then we'll tell her about St. Patrick's and the storm," his father said.

"You mean she doesn't know I've been gone?"

"No, son. We didn't want to upset her when she was still just recovering." His father looked at him long for a moment. "The Lord knew. There wasn't an hour went by without prayer for you and Zack."

"Thank you, Pa," Ben whispered, overcome by his feelings.

Whenever his father was especially happy, his laugh sounded as if it came from the ground up. It boomed out now as he clasped Ben in another bear hug, then turned to greet the captain.

The captain, leaning on his cane, ushered them all into the parlor. "I'm impressed with these two young men," he said. The conversation went on easily, with both Uncle Hiram and Ben's father joining in enthusiastically.

At last the captain rang for tea. With a sinking feeling Ben felt his stomach turn. What would Uncle Hiram and his pa think when they saw Letti? What would they do? The door opened shortly, but it was George carrying a tea tray who entered.

"Morning, Captain, gentlemen. Young miss is

took to her bed with the headache. Martha thought as how the tray was extra heavy, so I'd best be bringing it in."

"Thank you, George," Captain Sikes said.

Ben's thoughts whirled. Letti was avoiding being seen. He looked uneasily at his father and Uncle Hiram who were deep in conversation with the captain. What if they had discovered that Letti was here?

Only Zack and he and Colin knew about Letti, and Colin was gone, probably for good. His thoughts turned back to Letti. What if Letti didn't find Nat in time? He and Zack had promised to keep her secret, but now he wished with all his heart he had not made that promise.

11

Help Named Rosie

In the cellar of an old warehouse close to the waterfront, Letti's brother, Nat, lay crumpled in a miserable heap on the cold stone floor. The top hat he had been so proud of was gone. Thin sheets of ice covered what had once been puddles of water on the floor. Icicles hung from the inside of the window high above him. A small corner of the dirty window let in a bit of light where the snow had piled unevenly against the outside of the building.

His body shook uncontrollably for what seemed a long time before it stopped. Only now he could not feel his legs or his arms or the hunger pains that had plagued him earlier. He felt like he was floating bodyless. How long had he been here? Nat tried to remember.

Scenes from days ago flitted through his mind. The faces of the Plug Uglies who had taken him into the gang leered at him from beneath their tall black hats. They said he had to prove himself to the rest of them; then he would really be one of them. The faces were replaced suddenly by other dream faces, the older, meaner looking ones of the River Rats. What did they want with him? "No, no," he cried out, turning his head away as a knuckled fist struck at him.

"Letti's brother, right?" a leering voice jibed. "The River Rats don't take kindly to deserters. You can tell her that if you live long enough." Nat opened his eyes. He remembered the voice and then nothing else till he awakened stiff and bruised on the cellar floor.

Vaguely he recalled he had beat at the thick wooden door and vainly tried to budge it open. For a while, he thought, he had called and hollered for help, but all that seemed long ago. Nobody came. He had lost track of the days and nights. He was somewhere on the waterfront, that much he knew, but he might just as well have been at the bottom of the sea.

He turned onto his back and groaned. Fire in his head and throat shot through him. The foul ice on the floor made him retch when he sucked it, but it had slaked his burning throat, at least at first. Now it no longer helped, and he was too weak to make any effort.

"Letti," he whispered, "I know I been bad. I should'a gone with you to the mission." Letti's face hovered before his mind. He could never remember his mother. Letti had been the only family he really knew.

Her face appeared to Nat again; her dark eyes searched his. "Letti, I'm glad you went to the mission, but it's too late, Letti. Your Jesus won't have me now." Moaning feverishly, he fell into a shallow sleep troubled with dark shadowy figures. In the window above him where the sun had begun to melt the snow, a shaft of yellow light beamed down into the cellar and touched a corner of the prisoner's cell while Nat tossed unseeing.

Out on the street of warehouses and old tumbledown buildings above Nat, an occasional cart rolled heavily past, its driver unaware of the young victim in the dark cellar. Not many blocks away a newsboy and a boy in a thin jacket stood talking in earnest tones outside the office of the *Tribune*. The second boy was unmistakably Colin.

"If you ain't the lucky one," the newsboy said. "You show up here out of nowhere, riding first class back of a gentleman's sleigh what don't even know he's giving you a ride. And then old Dink gives you a job 'cause he likes your spunk in asking." The boy slapped his leg in glee. "Course, you didn't know two of his regulars got laid low with the fever pretty bad, and Dink just got the word he's needing to hire."

"Yup," Colin agreed. "Guess I'm the lucky one. You suppose they'll take me in at the Newsboys' Home for a bit?"

The newsboy nodded. "You being one of us now, you can get in. It'll cost you ten cents a night for a bed, supper, and a good hot wash. If you ain't got ten cents, I'll stand for you till you gets your first pay, seeing as how Dink asked me to show you the ropes." The boy slapped Colin on the shoulder, and together they moved on down the street.

At first Colin had fidgeted in the fresh, bright, sanitary atmosphere at the Newsboys' Home. He could pay his own way, thanks to his friend, but it was still strange to him that he had a bed to call his own, even a small locker for his things. After supper the fellows gathered in the classroom to listen to Mr. Smith, one of the teachers, read a Bible story. Without ever meaning to, Colin found himself listening intently. That David fellow was something to hear about, what with killing a bear with nothing but a slingshot.

The house routine was rigid. The rules held for all, including the one about listening to Mr. Smith read each night. After his second night Colin sort of took to the way things were. A fellow could go far, like Mr. Smith said, if he really wanted to make something of himself.

With change in his pocket, a full stomach, and a good night's sleep, Colin felt ten feet tall as he walked down Cherry Street.

Across the street, the slight figure of a girl, whose thin shawl was wrapped tightly about her shoulders, hesitated, then broke into a glad whoop. "Colin, is it yourself for real now?" the girl shouted.

"Rosie O'Neil, is it you?" Colin called back, and hurried over to where she stood. "Of all the luck," he said. "Who'd have thought we'd be running into each other again?"

"Looks like you're doing grand for yourself these days, Colin," Rosie said. "I never expected you to show up. Figured your luck had run out back last winter when you disappeared."

"You look okay yourself, Rosie," Colin said. He noted the girl's thinness and the pallor of her skin but knew it would not please her to mention it. "I'm just off to the baker's for some hot rolls. Treat's on me. Come on, and we'll catch up on old times."

Carefully Rosie forced herself to answer in the same casual manner Colin had offered. She would never let him know how long it had been since she had eaten a hot roll or any roll, for that matter.

Three quarters of an hour later Rosie left, having eaten four rolls to Colin's three. Her heart was full, too, of the promise to meet her old friend at the bakery in the morning. He said he planned to stop for rolls every morning now that he was employed. The thought of eating hot rolls two days in a row made her giddy. She hurried along the street with a lighter step.

In the back of her mind what Colin had told her about Letti and her brother, Nat, nagged at her. Those two had camped out down at the old theater with the rest of them at one time. She had heard the rumor that Nat was a Plug Ugly now and had run into trouble with the River Rat gang.

Suddenly she remembered something one of the younger girls had said about seeing a Plug Ugly being dragged into the cellar of one of the warehouses on Fletcher Street near the waterfront. The girl had fallen asleep in a deserted doorway hidden behind a post and awakened when she heard the commotion. Tomorrow she would tell Colin, sort of like a payment for the rolls.

In the morning, true to her word, Rosie waited for Colin by the bakery door. The odor of hot bread that wafted out into the street whenever anyone opened the door was almost too much for her empty stomach. She had had nothing since yesterday morning besides black tea and a hard crust shared with the others. Times were hard, and pickings were lean. It was all she could do sometimes to stay out of the grasp of the officers who patrolled the streets looking for vagrants to snatch. Of course, they couldn't patrol all the streets, and she had been lucky so far.

When Colin came whistling a tune, it was all Rosie could do to keep from dragging him into the bakery. Instead she smiled at him, not wanting to press her luck. It was after the third roll that she told him about Nat and the River Rat gang.

Colin looked at her with a serious, searching look. "Do you think your friend could show me the place where they took Nat?" he asked.

"Could be for a price, she might," Rosie answered. "But if he's still there, and the River Rats ain't posted a guard, you'd be better off finding him yourself. The less attention you draw the better."

She was right. Colin knew that he didn't dare let any of the gang find out what he was up to, though what that was he didn't really know yet. "How many warehouses could there be on Fletcher Street, anyway?" he said.

"And how many across the way from a doorway with a post where somebody could fall asleep out of sight?" Rosie added.

"You plan on going there yourself?" she asked anxiously.

"Can't chance it now that I'm working. At least not today." He was puzzled. What could he do?

"Maybe you ought to get word to Letti," Rosie suggested. "If she's working for Marm Mandelbaum, it might be she can figure out a way to get him loose. If it's not too late already."

An idea came to Colin. "Listen," he said. "I ain't forgotten how to write some. If I write a note, will you take it for me? You'll have to hang around the mission till you see a kid with light brown curly hair and blue eyes. He's about my height only he's a preacher's kid, wears good clothes and all. His friend is a colored kid, a little taller than me. The first one's Ben; the other one's Zack. They sometimes come to the mission with Ben's aunt to help out." Colin stopped to see how much Rosie had taken in.

"Okay," she said. "So what do I have to do?"

"I don't know for sure if they'll come or not, but it's a chance we've got to take," Colin said. "But I tell you what. You stand guard in case they do, and I'll see that there's something in it for you, and that's a promise."

Rosie's eyes lit with the thought of the promised windfall. "Sure and I will, Colin," she said. He produced a stub of a pencil and proceeded to write something on a piece of torn-off newspaper packing.

"Just give it to Ben, but don't let anyone else see you do it."

Rosie tucked the note deep inside her dress pocket. "I'll wait today and tomorrow, too, if they don't come today." In her heart she regretted immediately that there would be no rolls on the morrow in that case.

"Here," Colin said, thrusting two pennies into her hand. "Take these and buy yourself some rolls on your way if you do have to watch tomorrow. You know where to find me at the Newsboys' Home."

What a piece of luck, Rosie thought as she watched Colin hurry off. In a way, she didn't really mind hanging around the mission, though she had never set foot inside. Besides that, she had a job. The sun was shining, and her Irish heart felt a song coming on, a ditty she had picked up somewhere on the streets.

12

A Secret No More

Icy slush clogged the gutters and collected in the streets. In spite of the winter sun, Rosie's thin shoes and shawl gave her little protection from the cold. At first she had stood against a wall and kept her eyes fastened on the mission across the street. With a certain smugness she watched the day school children enter the wide mission door. Some of them she knew by sight. They were a ragtag lot. For a minute she pictured herself walking through the mission door. "It must be daft I'm going," she told herself, "to dream of sitting inside some stuffy schoolroom with the likes of them." The truth of it was, she had heard the stories about indentured apprentices and their hard lives. Children with no parents to keep them might be sent off to work for some mean old master. And hadn't she seen with her own eyes one of the orphan trains that took children out west? Pack you off for a profit, them mission folks could. Then where would a body be?

She stamped her feet, flailed her arms, peered up and down the street, and went back to observing those who entered the mission and those who left. One of those who passed her was a lady dressed in fashionable clothes of brightly colored rich cloth that made Rosie stare. The woman smiled warmly at Rosie before she opened the mission door.

Two hours later the young woman came out again. This time she looked at Rosie, who was still doing her job of waiting. The woman drew closer and spoke. "Would you like to go inside where it's warmer?" she asked.

Rosie shook her head emphatically. "Any minute now, me brother is coming," she lied.

"I see," the woman said. "Well, perhaps another time." She smiled kindly and walked away.

For as long as she was in sight Rosie watched the woman. She might have been an angel with golden hair and her wings hidden under the thick woolen cloak she wore. Rosie's curiosity was aroused. What did the woman do in the mission? She might stake out the place, once her job was done, just to find out. Maybe she would take up the woman's invitation and have herself a look. Of course, now she had her job to do. Slapping her arms against her sides to keep warm she returned to her watch.

She began to think maybe Colin had been wrong. No one of Ben or Zack's description had showed. At four she would call it quits for the day.

The church bells had just rung half past two when three figures turned onto the street. One was a boy who fit Colin's description of Zack, the other Ben's. The third, a girl with red hair, left her blank. Maybe the girl was the aunt Colin had mentioned. She was sure of the other two as they drew near the mission. The girl carried a large basket, and each of the boys bore boxes.

As the girl opened the mission door, Rosie went into action. Quick as a cat she slipped up to Ben and held out Colin's note. "You Ben?" she asked. Without waiting for an answer she shoved the note at him. "Colin sent you this." Like a streak she ran off, leaving a bewildered Ben behind her.

"Colin," Ben called after her. "Do you know where he is?" But it was no use; the girl never looked back and was soon out of sight. Ben opened the note to read it.

Abigail let go of the door. "What's going on?" She peered at the note Ben was trying to read.

"Tell Leti to look in warhase celer on Fletcha cross frum door with post. Be kareful. Colin."

"It's from your friend Colin," Abigail cried, "the one you said saved your lives."

"It sounds to me like Colin's found Letti's brother," Ben said.

"You know where Fletcher Street is?" Zack asked Abigail.

"I think it's down near the waterfront. We drove that way once to pick up something for the mission," she answered. "Do you think that's where the gang is holding Letti's brother?"

Ben and Zack had tried to keep Letti's secret, but Abigail had overheard them talking about Letti and the captain. She had promised not to tell so long as they let her help look for Nat.

"It must be the place," Ben said. "Why else would Colin have sent this note?"

Abigail shifted her basket; then in a voice that defied challenge she announced, "We'll deliver these things and go straight there for a look. Nobody will bother us. It's just a street full of warehouses. This time of year there won't be anything much going on down there. It's the only clue we have. If Nat is being held there, we need to find out quickly."

Ben groaned. Not again. He had promised himself the last time in Five Points that he would never go back without an adult. The waterfront didn't sound any better. What if the River Rats gang did hang out there?

Zack walked in step with Ben a little behind Abigail, who had stubbornly headed directly for the waterfront when they came out of the mission. "I'm telling my legs," he said to Ben. 'Legs, you be ready to run on the double if I say go.'"

Ben nodded, too sobered by the thought of what lay ahead to laugh. "It could come to that," he agreed. They walked the rest of the way in silence. It was almost four. These days it would be dark early. Ben quickened his pace.

Fletcher Street was deserted—no houses, no businesses, only warehouses. "At least it's not a long street," Abigail said cheerfully. "Now, what did your friend mean by a door with a post in it?"

From where they stood the doors on either side of the street looked dark and old. Some of them were large enough to draw a horse and wagon through. There were hitching posts along the way, but no such thing as a door with a post in it.

They were almost down to the end of the street when Zack said, "Ain't that a door with a hitching post right in front?" He pointed to the next-to-last doorway. The stone post was one of those thick ones with carvings sprouting out from each side and a trough built into the front. Directly across from it loomed a large wooden building as lifeless and dark as all the rest of the buildings on the street. The three crossed over warily.

"Let's walk to the end of the block. If anybody's here they'll think we're just passing by," Ben said.

At the corner they turned, glanced back, then continued toward the back of the warehouses. There was still no sign of anyone. Behind the second warehouse in, Ben stopped. "Abigail, you stand guard. If anybody comes, let us know. Zack, we'll split up. You take the left, and I'll go 'round the right side. Maybe there's a window or something we can see in to the cellar."

Abigail gripped Ben's sleeve. "If you hear me whistle good and loud, you come running," she said.

"Right," Ben agreed.

This time it was Ben who found the small window facing east where the morning sun had melted away some of the snow. Zack, having found nothing, returned as Ben cautiously approached the window. Together, one on each side, they tried to see inside.

After a few seconds Ben pressed his forehead against the pane. It was hard to see anything. Evidently the window had been built high up and just large enough for use as a coal chute.

Zack rubbed the snow clear from his side, shaded his eyes with his hand, and peered intensely into the gloom below. As he watched, something white moved, stopped, then moved again. Zack let his eyes focus. Slowly the outline of what he saw made sense. "That's got to be him," he whispered. "He's down there all right."

Kneeling next to Zack, Ben strained to see where Zack pointed. A heap of rags lay on the floor. It moved and turned a pale face toward them and away again. "It's him. It has to be," Ben said.

"Ain't nobody else down there, far as I can see," Zack added. "You reckon we can get him out of there?"

"Better tell Abigail what we've found," Ben said. "From the looks of him, I think it's going to take more than the two of us to get him out." His attempts to loosen the window frame hadn't budged it. "We'll have to break the glass to get in. There's no sign of anybody around, but we can't be sure. Wait a minute while I tell Abigail."

Zack watched the figure below move slightly as if in pain. In a flash Ben was back with Abigail. Crouching, she peered into the small window and let out a gasp.

"What if they've killed him?" she moaned.

"He may be hurt, but he's not dead," Ben said. "We saw him move."

"We've got to get help," Abigail urged. "The police or someone."

"All right," Ben said. "But somebody has to stay here in case the gang comes back and moves him." He looked around for somewhere to hide. The bleak yard offered no cover that he could see.

Zack stood up. "You two go. I can stay here with him."

"But what if the gang comes back?" Abigail wailed.

Zack looked about him for a stout stick or something to defend himself, useless as it might be against a gang, but there was nothing. He straightened, thought a moment, and said, "What about that post 'cross the street? I can hunker down behind it and watch from there. That way, if they come I can spot 'em. Besides, it's gettin' dark, and I reckon it won't be so easy to spot me."

Zack was right. The sun was going down fast. They would have to hurry before the gang did come back. Ben wanted desperately to stay with Zack, but he couldn't let Abigail return alone. "We'll be back," he said. "You stay low, Zack, you hear?"

"I'll be here waitin'," Zack answered. Ben and Abigail watched him cross to the post, saw him hunch down behind it, and then took off running. Zack was alone with the lengthening shadows on the deserted street of warehouses.

Abigail, a good runner, kept up well with Ben.

"To the mission," she shouted to Ben. "It's closer. We can get help there."

With the waterfront and its warehouses behind them, the neighborhood changed to houses, small shops, and grungy saloons. There were people about, but neither Abigail nor Ben stopped to ask for help. In this section of town where minding one's own business was the habit of most of the residents, they were unlikely to receive any.

At last, out of breath and barely able to speak, Abigail followed Ben into the mission whose outer doors were not yet locked for the night.

The young man behind the desk looked up in surprise, then hurried out to them. "Why, Miss Abigail, what's wrong? You look as if you'd been chased here by a pack of wild dogs."

"Please," Abigail said half sobbing, "you've got to help us. It's Letti's brother. We found him, but he's hurt, and we can't get him out. Oh, please, hurry."

"Just a minute while I get Mr. Thurston. Sit down, both of you, and catch your breath." The young man hurried out of the room. Before Ben could think what they ought to do next, the young man returned with a middle-aged man who looked for all the world like a broad-shouldered sailor Ben had known at home.

"Now lassie, what's this you and the laddie are so troubled about?" he asked.

Between them Abigail and Ben poured out their story as quickly as they could.

When they were through, Mr. Thurston was already on his feet and heading for his coat. "We must go there at once," he said. "Matron will see that you are escorted home safely, Miss Abigail. I think your father should be informed."

To Ben's surprise, Abigail did not argue. Meekly she said, "Yes, sir. That will give Mother and me time to prepare a room for the boy. You will bring him to us, won't you? I know Mother will want him there for Letti's sake."

"Your mother's a fine nurse, lassie. I canna think of a better place for the lad. Go along and tell her to expect us." With that he was out the front door. One arm about Ben's shoulders propelled him forward.

They were in luck. A passing coachman eager for a fare stopped at Mr. Thurston's shout. "To Fletcher Street, sir, and hurry," Mr. Thurston boomed. "Never you worry, lad, we'll make it. The Lord is a present help in time of trouble."

The cheerfulness of Mr. Thurston's voice and the powerful build of the man somehow went together in a comforting way. Ben leaned back as the cabby raced down the street. Free for the moment, he began to think of Zack waiting for them. What if the gang had come back? What if they had seen Zack? A shudder passed over him.

As if he had sensed it, Mr. Thurston looked at Ben. "This is a time for prayer, lad," he said.

In the dark street behind his post, Zack sat straining to hear the sound of feet or voices. Once, the wind sent something scurrying and made him jump. It was nothing but an old piece of newspaper. Had he been here an hour? What could be taking Ben so long? Why had he stayed, anyway? If the gang came back, what could he do besides watch? Suppose Letti's brother really did die down there; what good would it be staying here?

High above in the dark sky a faint star shone. Zack traced it with his finger. "Lord, that your star up there," he whispered. "Almost forgot you looking down here all the time, Lord. Feels good knowing that." Mistress Capp had read him that right out of the Bible. For a few minutes Zack forgot where he was and remembered things the old lady had taught him. "Like she said, the Lord don't know the difference between day and night. It's all the same to him."

When the carriage came rushing 'round the corner and pulled up, Zack thought his heart had stopped. Within seconds Ben was at his side, pulled him to his feet, and dragged him over to the carriage.

Between the driver and Mr. Thurston the cellar door opened. Its rusted lock had given way under the blows of the driver's iron tool. In seconds they were inside. By the light of the driver's lamp they found Nat.

"More dead than alive, he looks," the driver said anxiously.

Together the men lifted the boy's limp body from the icy floor.

Mr. Thurston wrapped his coat about the boy and

took him in his arms. "Aye, there's breath in him yet, but it's a warm bed and loving hands he's needing."

As they left the cellar, Ben shivered. How long had Nat been there in its bone-chilling cold? Beside him Zack shook his head with the same wonder. Outside, the night air was sharp, but somehow not as cold as the cellar. Overhead a few stars had joined the first shining one.

On the ride home, Mr. Thurston held Nat's head against his chest tenderly as one might hold a small child. At his uncle's house Ben's father took the bundle that was Nat and bore him to the waiting bed.

Mr. Thurston went at once to fetch the doctor. Abigail, her eyes a telltale red, came into the hallway.

"Did you see how white he looks?" she said. "Poor Letti. Papa's gone to send a message to Captain Sikes on the telegraph. He knows all about Letti now." She faltered as she looked first at Ben, then at Zack. "I had to tell him. Uncle Stewart, too."

"Would have done it myself, anyway," Ben said.

"Right," Zack added.

The front door opened, and Ben's uncle strode into the hallway. "Well, I've done all I could. The wires must be down at the captain's. I'm afraid I couldn't get through to let Letti know about her brother. We'll go first thing in the morning to fetch her back."

A feeling like a prickle ran through Ben's mind. If the wires were down, that meant the captain and

Letti were alone in the house with just the two old people. They had had no way to call for help if Marm's men did show up. And Letti wouldn't know about Nat. If she thought the gang still had Nat, what then?

13

An Honorable Wound

At Captain Sikes's home soft yellow light glowed from an upstairs study window in the west wing and from the small room that was Letti's in the lower east wing. Martha and George had long since gone to their rooms above the kitchen to sleep peacefully in the gentle darkness that wrapped the rest of the house.

Letti sat on her bed stitching a seam in the skirt she intended to wear in the morning. Tomorrow George would take her to town for the shopping Martha wanted done. She would have to plan her time carefully if she hoped to find out anything about Nat.

The sound of pebbles against her window startled her. Maybe Colin had come back, but why? With her candle in hand she hurried to see.

The face in the window was not Colin's. Letti stifled her gasp with one hand. Outside, the leering grin of Pigeye, one of Marm's runners, flattened against the glass. He motioned with his hand for Letti to open the window.

Trembling, she set her candle on the floor and

lifted the window a few inches. Pigeye forced it higher so that they were face-to-face.

"What do you want?" Letti hissed. "You're taking a chance coming round here before the captain's even gone to his bed," she scolded.

"I'm doing me job, and you better be doing yours," Pigeye answered roughly. "Marm wants the layout now."

"I wasn't expecting you tonight, and I ain't wrote anything yet," Letti answered.

"Don't need no writing," Pigeye said and tapped his head. "I keeps it all up here. Just you start talking, beginning with what's inside the front door."

Hopelessly Letti drew a mental map of the house for Pigeye and answered his questions as briefly as she could. He demanded to know where the captain kept his silver and what kinds of locks they would run into if any. Letti did her best to stall him, but it was no use.

"Listen here, me girl," he said ruthlessly. "You make one false step, and we'll cut your throat."

Letti nodded. "But you got to let me know when you're coming so I can be ready," she said.

Pigeye grinned at her. "As to that, you won't have much sleep tonight. You be ready at midnight. You know the signal—three circles with the candle in your window. Soon's we're certain the captain's snoring in his bed you open the front door and we'll do the rest."

Letti's heart sank, but she managed to whisper,

"Right, then, but mind you do your job so's nobody gets hurt. I ain't into murder."

Pigeye snorted. "Two old people and an invalid? It's a pushover. Besides, if they do get in the way, you know Marm's rule: no witnesses. If they're lucky, they won't even wake up till it's all over. So long as you stay on the right side of Marm you don't need to worry. Marm'll take care of her own. You can count on that."

He had mistaken Letti's fears for the captain and the old folks as fear for her own safety. Letti let it go and nodded. When Pigeye was gone she lowered the window. For a long time she sat on the side of the bed lost in the terrible fear that had suddenly swept down upon her.

What had she done? How could she get out of it now? What if the captain did wake, or George came down in the midst of the thieving? She looked at her own hands. A thief's hands. They were scrubbed clean, and on her right thumb was a callous from all the peeling she had done to help Martha with the leathery skinned winter apples. After tonight she would have to leave the captain's. Marm would want her somewhere else for another job if they were successful tonight. She didn't doubt that they would be.

Somewhere a clock chimed the hour of ten. How long had she sat there? The room had grown chilly, and Letti wrapped her shawl about her shoulders. In two hours Marm's men would be back waiting for her to let them in. They would steal every valuable thing in sight as well as the silver. Would they bring a sack for her to fill? She looked again at her hands pressed together in her lap almost as if to pray. She'd seen praying hands in a picture at the mission.

Abigail's mother had shown her that picture. "Anyone can have hands like that," she had said. "God loves us so much he wants us to pray, to talk to him."

Everything seemed so clear back then, Letti thought. Now that she had turned back to her old ways, there was no use praying. If only Nat had gone with her to the mission everything would be all right now.

Big tears filled her eyes and splashed down her cheeks as she slid to the floor and leaned her head against the bed. Maybe she never should have run away from Abigail's house. Her whole body shook with sobs. She felt small and alone. She needed help. Without realizing it, Letti found herself praying.

"So you see how it is, Lord. I don't want nothing to happen to the captain or George and Martha, but there's Nat, and I don't know what to do." After a few moments, Letti's tears stopped, and a calmness settled down inside her. There was only one right thing to do.

Quietly she stepped into the hallway with a fresh candle in her hand. At the top of the stairs she turned right and made her way to the captain's room.

It was several minutes before her light knock brought a bewildered, sleepy looking Captain Sikes in a rumpled dressing gown to the door. "Lizzie, what is it? Is someone ill?" he asked.

"Sir, we're in trouble for sure, and it's all my fault. I've got to tell you before it's too late," Letti said urgently.

The captain opened the door wide and pointed toward his sitting room. He poked at the fire until it flared up brightly. "That's better," he said. "Now tell me what this is all about."

"First off, my name ain't Lizzie, it's Letti." As Letti explained, the captain listened intently and stopped to question her at several points. When she was through he paced the room, limping slightly on his wounded leg.

Letti couldn't bear the sight and began to cry.

The captain stopped pacing. "Look at me, Letti," he commanded.

Her face burned with shame as she raised her eyes to meet his.

"I believe you, Letti. What you did was wrong, but I think you did the only thing you could think of in the circumstances." The captain patted her head. "It took a lot of courage to come to me. Now, Letti, the first thing we have to do is telegraph for help, and I promise you, I'll do everything in my power to see to your brother's rescue."

Letti looked horrified. "But they'll have cut the wires. It's the first thing they do when they come to lay out a job. Pigeye would have done it when he came to give me the word."

It was true. A quick check by the captain showed

the worst. The wires were indeed down. It was almost eleven o'clock, too late to ride into town for help. The captain looked worried, then determined.

"Well, they shan't find us sleeping, thanks to you," he said. "I have my rifle, and we have the advantage of surprise on our side. Will you help me, Letti?"

"With my life, sir," she answered. Her fears seemed to have evaporated suddenly. "Shall I fetch George and Martha, sir?"

"I wish we needn't, but I think if there is going to be gunfire they'd best be warned. George can help me while you stay with Martha. But first, Letti, we shall have to let them in just the way it was planned. Can you do it?"

"I can, sir," Letti answered.

"Good," the captain said. "Then you must tell them to wait for a minute while you fetch the key to the silver closet. As soon as you are out of the hallway into the kitchen George and I will surprise them. You and Martha lock the door and stay upstairs until it's over."

When Letti returned with George, dressed hastily in his stable clothes, the captain was clothed in his army uniform. A rifle and a Colt revolver lay on the dressing table next to their ammunition boxes.

"Thieves, is it!" George exclaimed. "We'll give them something to remember, Captain." In his hand George held an ancient hunting rifle.

It was almost midnight. Letti stood trembling at her bedroom window with the lighted candle in her hand. As the clock struck twelve she held the candle high, then moved it in a wide circle three times. She could see nothing outside in the dark this time. All the same, she knew that Marm's boys were out there. Her heart pounded as she raced to the front door.

Slowly, without making a sound, Letti opened the door. Three dark figures slipped past her into the hallway, one of whom she recognized as Pigeye.

"I've brought you a bag, my girl," he whispered. "Now give us the key and get busy."

"The key's in my apron pocket. Wait here while I fetch it," Letti whispered back.

Pigeye grabbed her arm in a tight hold. "You were supposed to have the key with you. Now get it and be fast about it." He turned to the other two men with him. "Johnny, you know the layout. Get them pictures off the dining room walls. Frames is worth plenty. And Billy, you start cleaning out the parlor."

Letti hesitated. This was all wrong. They were supposed to be together for the captain to surprise them. Quickly she stepped back toward the kitchen and screamed for the captain.

"Why, you little . . ." the angry voice of Pigeye began but stopped as Captain Sikes and his gun stood before them in a sudden blaze of light. Instinctively Pigeye had whipped out his knife and slashed at Letti before she could move. Now he stood with his knife in the air. Blood dripped down the blade. Marm's other two boys had stopped dead in their tracks with looks of sheer surprise on their faces.

"Drop it or I'll shoot it off," Captain Sikes said coolly. The knife in Pigeye's hand clattered to the floor.

"Now turn around, put your hands behind your heads, and face up against the wall, pronto," the captain commanded. "George, bring the rope and start with their ankles. If any of you so much as moves, I'll shoot. And I shoot equally well with the Colt in my left hand and the rifle in my right."

Letti's voice rang out. "And if the captain's guns ain't enough, I've one here that'll blow a hole through a barn." She held George's old hunting rifle.

George hurried to his task. "Now, if there's one thing I'm plum good at it's hog-tying." Within minutes all three of the thugs were securely hobbled in such a way that none of them could move.

Letti felt giddy with relief. "Now what, Captain?"

"Good work, Letti," Captain Sikes said and leaned heavily against a narrow table. Suddenly his face looked peculiar. He came toward Letti with both hands out. "Your arm's been cut," he said.

Letti stared down at her right arm that had only now begun to feel warm and sticky. Blood oozed from a slash above the elbow. She hadn't even known that Pigeye's knife had struck home. Within half an hour Martha's loving hands had cleaned and bandaged the flesh wound and made hot tea for the four of them.

In spite of her fears for Nat, Letti had never been happier. For once in her life she had done the right thing.

"Letti, that was the bravest thing I've ever seen anyone do," the captain said.

"It's an honorable wound you've got in action," George added.

Their words were like music to Letti's tired ears. The sound of the door knocker brought them all to shocked attention.

The knocking outside was insistent. "Police! Open up! I say, Captain Sikes, are you all right in there?" It was indeed the police, three of them. Abigail's uncle was with them.

"I don't know who sent you," the captain said, "but you're just in time to collect a pack of thieves caught red-handed."

"Once we learned that Letti was here we tried to reach you, sir, over the telegraph to tell you about Nat. When we found the wires were down we planned to come out in the morning. Only after Ben told us what might be happening here, with the wires down and all, the officers did some checking. The wires had been deliberately cut."

Abigail's uncle turned to Letti, who had remained seated on a kitchen chair under the insistence of Martha. Gently he broke the news. "I thought it best to come along with the officers and tell you about Nat myself, Letti. I'm afraid, child, that your brother is a pretty sick lad."

Letti looked at the captain. "Can I go, sir?"

The captain nodded, his voice almost too choked to speak. "Go with my prayers, Letti."

Letti didn't mean to fall asleep, but the carriage ride home proved too much for her. She never felt the arms that lifted her from the carriage nor the hands that put her to bed in her old bed next to Abigail's. She did not even awaken when someone bent to kiss her forehead.

14

Nat Goes Home

Abigail moved quietly so that she would not awaken Letti. She had dressed and was about to open the door when Letti stirred.

"Abby?" she said and sat up in bed. Her thick hair fell in a tumbled mass about her shoulders, and her eyes were wide with fear.

"Oh, Letti," Abigail cried. She ran to her friend and hugged her. "I'm so sorry. Can you ever forgive me for doubting you?" Tears flowed, and she hid her face against Letti's shoulder. She felt Letti wince and drew back immediately. "I forgot about your wounded arm. Does it pain you much?"

"Only a little," Letti said. "I don't mind it, really. Captain Sikes called it my badge of honor. Abby, I ain't done much in the way of honorable lately. I wanted to tell you, but everything just got out of hand before I knew it, and then I just couldn't." She reached for Abigail with her good arm to pull her close. With tears and broken words the girls comforted each other.

When Abigail finally sat back to dry her eyes she said, "You'll want to see Nat. While you dress, I'll fetch something for you to eat." Lovingly she smoothed Letti's pale forehead, then rose and hurried to her task.

In Nat's room the curtains had been opened to let in the morning sun. His white face, so frail it seemed his spirit was already showing through, looked like a small boy's against the pillows of the large bed. By his side Ben's father knelt where he had been all night. Nat's thin hand lay cupped in Ben's father's large ones.

When Letti entered the room it was with a heavy heart. She knew from Abby that the doctor feared Nat had pneumonia. Nat's eyes were closed, and for a moment Letti felt faint. Was she too late?

Ben's father looked up and in a voice weary but full of gentleness comforted her at once. "He is still with us, Letti. Come and sit by him so that when he wakes it will be your face he sees."

Letti sat in the chair offered her. Ben's father quietly left the room. Carefully Letti touched Nat's hand. It was warm. She brushed the thick curls gently back from his forehead. He didn't stir, and holding his limp hand in hers she waited.

Abigail's mother had come in to stand by Letti. At the sight of her Letti's tears spilled over once again. "Oh, ma'am," she whispered choking back sobs.

Quickly Aunt Hett enveloped her in her arms and drew her head against her. With soothing words she comforted Letti. When the tears had stopped, she kissed her and dried her face with her apron corner. "Now, love, you stay with Nat, and I'll bring you tea. The doctor will be back later this morning, but the best thing for Nat is having you here," she said.

Letti nodded, smoothed her skirt and cap, and took Nat's hand once more.

"That you, Letti?" The weak voice was Nat's. His open eyes looked at her.

"I'm right here," Letti said as cheerfully as she could. "I don't plan on leaving you, either, till you're up and about, so there."

Nat was silent for a moment. His eyes searched as if he expected someone else. "Is he gone?" he whispered.

"Who?" Letti asked anxiously. She looked around, then back at Nat.

"The preacher," Nat said. "He was watching for me. I like that, Letti. And when the angels come for me, he said, I don't have nothin' to fear. I'm all clean inside now, Letti, and I belong to Jesus just like you." He stopped while a deep cough racked him, and Letti raised his head to ease him. As she laid him back onto the pillows, he whispered, "I'm going there soon. It'll be so grand." Nat's pale face seemed to glow with the picture in his mind. "I wish you was coming, too, Letti," he said weakly.

She could barely speak. Mustering all her strength, she said, "Natty, Natty. I'm so glad for you. And don't you worry none. I'll be coming, too, and you just wait for me, you hear?" Her voice broke. She grasped Nat's hand to her lips and covered it with kisses.

Quietly Ben's father had returned to kneel by the bedside with his wife next to him. They were all here now. Abigail and her mother and father stood at the foot of the bed with Ben and Zack.

Letti knew in her heart what each of them had known. Nat was dying, and it was too late to save him. Still she kept her eyes on his face and held his hand to give him strength.

Nat's eyes turned to Ben's father, and he tried to smile. In a voice so low that Letti could barely hear him he said, "Tell me again about heaven."

Ben's father took Nat's other hand in his, then in a strong and steady voice began to sing the simple hymn "There Is a Happy Land." One by one the others joined in, softly singing the well-known words. Ben's face streamed with tears as he tried to sing.

Before the song was finished, Nat slipped away to see for himself the wonders of that land. He was gone, but Letti, brokenhearted, could not let go of his hand. After a while the family formed a tight circle with arms about each other and Letti. Then Ben's father prayed for the little wanderer without a home who was home at last.

When they finished praying, Ben's uncle, whose big voice was now gentle, said, "I'll let the mission know to arrange for Nat's burial." Letti could only nod as the family led her from the room.

Ben's mother and his aunt stayed behind to prepare the young body whose spirit had now left it.

15

A Sudden Change of Plans

On the morning of the funeral a little group gathered on the plot of burial land owned by the mission. Captain Sikes had paid for the coal for the fire needed to thaw the frozen ground so that a grave could be dug. The small wooden coffin now lay in its place. Above it Ben's father stood with bent head to give the final benediction. As a last tribute to Nat the family and a few mourners who had joined them sang the very hymn they had sung at Nat's bedside, "There Is a Happy Land."

Some of the older children from the mission had come to the funeral with two of the volunteer ladies. Word had spread among others of the Five Points. A few curious street urchins pressed in behind the mission folks to watch the event. Among them stood Colin with Rosie close behind him.

Rosie was delighted to see that the lady with the beautiful clothes had come with the mission children. Curiosity gripped her. Maybe tomorrow she would chance a look inside the mission just to see what it was the lady did. It struck her as strange that all these people would come to the burial of a

street boy. As the lady accepted a snow-white handkerchief from a young captain in army uniform,
Rosie dashed away a tear of her own.

After the service Ben, who had spotted Colin, hurried over with Zack to greet him. "Never thought
we'd see you here," Ben said.

With a proud look Colin said, "I'm a newsboy
now, you know. Can't always get away, but I heard
about Nat. I'm right sorry."

Abigail and Letti walked together toward the
boys. Letti looked pale and sad. She held out her
hand to Colin. "I know that you were the one who
helped us find Nat. Thanks, Colin," she said.

Colin held her hand for a moment, then tipped
his hat. He swallowed hard. "I only wish it'd been
sooner."

Letti nodded. Silently the boys watched as she
went with Abigail to the waiting carriage.

"She's feeling powerful lonesome," Zack said.
Turning back to Colin his eyes lit with welcome.
"How you doing, Colin?" he asked. "You staying
'round here now?"

Colin beamed. "Ain't never had it better," he
said. "I bunk down in the Home for Newsboys, a
swell place. A fellow can eat and still save a bit living there. Might get back to schooling along the
way soon's I can."

Ben's fears for Colin faded. He would be all right.
The carriages were waiting, and Colin had business
elsewhere. The last Ben saw of him was a jaunty
wave of the hand as he disappeared around a corner.

On the day following the funeral, the household, not yet recovered, received another blow. Though Captain Sikes had not pressed any charges against Letti, the three arrested men swore that Letti had put them up to it in the first place.

"A sorry business, this," the officer who came for Letti said. "I'm afraid I'll have to take the young miss downtown with me."

Aunt Hett was indignant. "Well, then, if you must, officer, I'll just be going right along with you. If this child has to spend the night in jail, then you'll have to put up with me too." Ben's father and his uncle were not at home to add their protests, but no amount of argument would persuade the officer from his duty. It was a flustered policeman who left the house with an indignant Aunt Hett holding firmly to Letti's hand.

Ben's mother stood in the doorway holding on to Susie, who screamed loudly for the bad policeman to bring back her mother and Letti. Ben and Zack ran for their jackets to take a hastily written note to Ben's uncle. Abigail was pale and speechless.

By late afternoon the captain appeared at the police station with a court order to release the prisoner. It was signed by Judge Solby, a personal friend of the captain's.

Within five minutes a red-faced Aunt Hett, holding onto Letti's hand, was brought to the waiting room.

Smiling broadly, Ben's uncle enveloped his wife

and Letti in a great bear hug. "I'm proud of you, woman," he roared.

Aunt Hett, a little flustered, straightened her hat. "The sooner we leave here, the better," she said.

"Now, ma'am, you were never rightly a prisoner," the officer in charge said. "It was all your own choice to accompany the girl."

"Humph," was all the answer Aunt Hett gave as she swept past him, still holding tightly to Letti.

Captain Sikes reassured them that though Letti would be asked to testify in private before the judge as soon as arrangements could be made, she was in no danger of being tried as an accomplice.

Letti could only thank him over and over. "I don't deserve your goodness," she cried.

The captain smiled at her fondly. "Child," he said, "your courage may have saved our lives. If you hadn't warned us in time I don't like to think what might have happened. Whatever mistakes you made before, you've wiped the slate clean."

At the house a tearful Abigail embraced Letti. For the next hour there were cakes, hot tea, and buttery biscuits in front of a blazing fire for all, including the captain.

Before the captain left he offered Letti her old job back. "We could use you, Letti. Martha's not young anymore, and the house is far too big."

Such kindness brought fresh tears to Letti's eyes, but she shook her head. "It's not that I don't thank you with all my heart," she said, "but I'm thinking there's something else I've got to do."

The captain didn't press her. He took his leave with a promise to fetch Letti himself on the appointed court day.

That night Ben lay awake thinking about Nat's funeral and Letti's arrest. "You awake?" he asked Zack.

"Yup," Zack answered. "Been lying here thinking. Feels like we been living here a lot longer than a few weeks."

"I know," Ben said. "Maybe it's because so much has happened. Guess it'll be kind of dull when we get home to Tarrytown. I reckon things will settle down here now that Letti's back." He yawned and closed his eyes.

Zack was still awake listening to Ben's soft snoring. He closed his eyes wearily. He couldn't quite get Letti's old gang, the River Rats, out of his mind. Well, whatever lay ahead, it could wait.

Zack had been right about Letti's old gang. During the night someone smeared red paint on the front of the house. In big bold letters they wrote "ONCE A THIEF ALWAYS A THIEF." Below was a crude skull and crossbones with a rat perched on top.

When the policeman who came to investigate was gone, Ben's father helped Uncle Hiram remove the paint. Inside, Aunt Hett comforted a distraught Letti.

"Don't fret, child," Aunt Hett said. "For a while we'll have to do as the officer suggested. I don't want you out of the house alone. All of us will keep a sharp eye. The police will be looking out, too, and soon whoever is behind this will find better things to do."

"They know I went to work for Marm's gang, and they think I'll be back again. Maybe I can't ever get away from the past," Letti wailed.

"You don't have to do it alone," Ben heard his father say.

"He's right, Letti, dear," Ben's mother added. "Hett and I both know it from experience." His mother glanced at Aunt Hett, who nodded. "Let us tell you what we mean," Ben's mother said. She put her arm about Letti's shoulder. Together the two sisters led Letti upstairs.

Ben looked at his father for an explanation. What was it that his mother and aunt knew from experience?

Uncle Hiram, who had been standing near the fire, poked the logs till bright orange flames caught the fresh log, then sat down again next to Zack. "You tell it, Stewart," he said.

"There are some things only your mother and aunt will ever know. Others I'll leave to them to tell. But when your mother was six and Hett was eight, their ma died of fever. After a year their pa took another wife to help raise the girls." Ben's father paused. "He was killed in an accident shortly afterward so he never knew what kind of stepmother he'd brought into the house."

Uncle Hiram added, "She was a mean-spirited woman who went to church on Sunday but made

life miserable for those girls the rest of the week."
He shook his head sadly.

Ben's father went on, "Your mother and Hett
never stopped believing what their real ma and pa
had taught them—that God would never forsake
them. It was hard at times, but there are no two
finer women today."

"What happened to the stepmother?" Ben asked.

Uncle Hiram answered, "By the time the girls
were old enough to be on their own, all that mean-
ness inside her finally wore her out. The girls tried
to help her, but she died without a word of kindness on her lips."

At supper Letti appeared calm, her hands steady
as she helped Abigail serve. She even smiled at
something Susie said. It seemed to Ben that whatever his mother and aunt had told Letti had worked.
Ben dug deeply into his blackberry pie. He was com-
pletely unprepared for his father's next words.

After clearing his throat, Ben's father announced,
"In all the events of these past two days, I clean forgot to tell you boys that I'll be leaving in the morning for a spell." Ben stopped eating to listen.

His father produced a folded letter from his vest.
"This came in the mail a few days ago. It seems
that the church board has decided my leave should
be permanent." Silence followed his statement.
"Now, Ben, your mother and I have discussed this,
and we think it's best all around. I'm not giving up
the ministry, just changing the place."

"But what will you do?" Ben asked. His head

swirled. If they returned to Tarrytown now, the problems would be bigger than the ones he thought they had left behind.

"Your folks will stay right here with us," Aunt Hett said cheerfully.

"Mr. Thurston has kindly asked your father to help at the mission until we're sure of where our next post will be," Ben's mother added.

"Will we be going back at all?" Ben asked. "And what about Zack?"

"One thing at a time, son," his father replied. "For the present I'd like you and your mother to stay here. I need to make some arrangements and finish a few loose ends. As for you, Zack, I see no reason why you shouldn't stay on till the end of the month as planned." He looked at Zack.

"Yes, sir," Zack said.

The blackberry pie lost its appeal as a sinking feeling took hold of Ben's insides. A few minutes ago his life had been one thing, and without notice everything had changed. And what about Zack? Ben wanted to say something, but he couldn't.

16

A Part of Growing

Ben's father was gone for almost a week. This morning large raindrops ran down the windowpanes to form little streams that met, widened, then broke away as Ben and Zack watched from their beds in the attic. Ben yawned lazily. The rain would keep them in today, he supposed.

"I been thinking, Ben," Zack said slowly. "Maybe I ain't going back to Tarrytown neither. You remember Chaplain Turner? We saw him in Cooper's Union the night of the big meeting."

Ben remembered the tall, handsome, colored soldier who had spoken to the crowd. "Sure, I recall him."

"Well," Zack continued, "I reckon I kind of had the idea that night when I saw the chaplain. I ain't sure they'll have me, but I'm thinking on joining the army. They say some of the drummer boys and camp aides that joined up last year ain't no bigger than me. I reckon they'd take me same as the others."

"That's crazy!" Ben said. He sat upright. "What do you want to do that for?" Without waiting for an answer, Ben realized he knew the reason. "I

149

guess it ain't really crazy, if that's what you want. I wish I could go with you, Zack."

Zack propped himself on one elbow and looked serious. "You know you can't join up with the colored troops. Course, you could find yourself a regiment. But what about your ma and pa? You all they got, Ben. It ain't likely they gonna let you go, specially now with your pa out of the church."

Ben didn't answer right away. When he did it was with a note of bitterness in his voice. "They can keep their old church," he said. "But I can't rightly leave pa now."

"And your ma too," Zack said. "Reckon if I had a ma like that I'd wait a spell, leastwise till I could leave with an easy mind. Sometimes it pays to be an orphan," he said, then grinned at Ben.

Ben didn't smile. If it hadn't been for the church board's asking his pa to leave, things would have worked out after a while. He and Zack could have gone back to their old ways. Ben tossed his pillow to the foot of the bed. If Zack's mind was made up, Ben knew there wasn't much use arguing. "You hungry?" he asked.

"Could do with a few of those fried cakes your Aunt Hett say she's plannin' to make this morning."

The rain that kept them in all day stopped toward evening just before Ben's father returned. For a few minutes Ben couldn't tell what it was that seemed different about his pa, but something was. He strode through the hallway to greet Ben's mother with a great bear hug. Susie insisted on being next, and he lifted her into the air, swinging her up over his head. As he lowered her safely to the floor he said, "Susie, my girl, I feel like a giant today."

With a ringing gladness in his voice he announced, "My dears, I believe God has good plans for us, and it's as if a weight's been lifted off my shoulders. There's a fine young man fresh out of seminary, a nephew of Mr. Brewster, who will take the church for the time being. And from what I can see, the board would have to be blind not to call him permanently. I can only thank the Lord for him." Gratefully he accepted the glass Uncle Hiram offered him. "Thanks, Hiram. It's been a long time since I've felt this free."

"Well, I can tell you, Stewart, the mission work is not easy, as you know, but there's no one we'd rather see there than yourself," Uncle Hiram said warmly.

"It will be an honor for me to work with those good people," Ben's father replied. "At least until we see what's ahead for us," he added.

"Until the way is clear to you, Stewart, Hett and I want you and the family to stay right here. We can't tell you what it has meant to us both having family close again."

"For the time being, anyway, we'll accept your kind offer," Ben's father said. "Our household goods will have to be stored, but I think we can work that out."

Before Aunt Hett called everyone to the evening meal, Ben knew from the way his father spoke as he talked about the mission that he could hardly wait to begin the new work. Well, his father might be happy to stay here, but living in his uncle's house wasn't Ben's idea of a home. And there was Zack.

During supper Ben watched his mother's face, but there was no hint of regret. If anything, she seemed glad. Aunt Hett was her sister, so he should have expected that. The conversation flowed on about all the bright possibilities ahead. Nobody asked Ben for his opinion.

It was late when Ben and Zack finally went to the attic for the night. Zack shut the door behind them and leaned against it. "I'll be going in the morning," he said quietly.

A cold stillness settled inside Ben.

"I've made up my mind, Ben. It's what I want to do. There's no sense my goin' back to Tarrytown when I don't figure on staying there."

Ben swallowed hard before he could speak. "If that's the way you want it, Zack," he said.

"Soon's folks are gone about their business in the morning, I'll slip out. That way there won't be any fussing."

Ben nodded. "You'll be wanting to pack your stuff tonight, I guess. I reckon the army'll give you a rifle," Ben said. "But you better take my hunting knife with you, anyway. It will give you something to remember me by." Ben took the leather pouch with the hunting knife out of the pack he kept it in and handed it to Zack.

"I don't need nothing to help me remember you,

Ben. You know that," Zack said. "But it's sure fine, and I'll take it if you'll take that Indian arrowhead you wanted." He removed a stone arrowhead from his pack and handed it to Ben.

Ben turned the arrowhead over in his hand. It was the one Zack had found last spring, a perfect specimen. "Thanks," he said. "I'd be proud to own it."

When Zack's things were stowed in his pack there was nothing more to do. Ben snuffed out the candle and lay still, thinking about all that had happened. "You write me, Zack," he commanded.

"I don't write fancy, but I reckon you'll make it out okay. And you write back, hear?" Zack said.

"You can count on it." In the dark Ben's face was wet with tears that spilled silently onto his pillow.

At breakfast Ben made a show of eating but slipped most of his share of biscuits into his pants pockets. After the men had gone to work, Ben and Zack waited until the women went upstairs. Abigail and Letti were busy in the kitchen. Zack had hidden his pack and jacket in the sitting room close to the front door.

"It's time," Zack said, picking up his pack. "I better be going before your ma or your aunt come down."

With his hand on the door handle Ben nodded. "I don't want you to go, Zack," he said. "I wish I was going with you."

"I know you do, Ben." Zack's face as he looked at his friend was all the farewell he could manage.

"Here," Ben said. "I almost forgot. These biscuits

will come in handy, and there's fare for the omnibus. You can owe me out of your first paycheck."

"I'll see that you get it back with interest, including some army hardtack." Zack grinned, then grew serious. "So long, Ben."

Ben opened the door. He waved as Zack turned once to look back. Slowly he shut the door against the cold. For a minute his hand lingered on the latch. He could not believe that Zack was gone. Then he was running blindly into the sitting room looking for anywhere to be alone. It was here that a short time later Letti discovered him crouched behind the sofa.

"That you, Ben?" Letti asked puzzled.

Not answering, Ben hastily dried his eyes before he sat up stiffly. He heard Letti shut the sitting room door. She returned to stand directly in front of him.

"What's the matter, Ben?" Letti demanded.

Ben turned his face away, but Letti wasn't impressed. Kneeling down, she lifted his chin and forced him to look at her.

"Where's Zack?" she asked.

Ben tried not to meet her eyes, as he said, "He's gone. Zack is gone."

"What do you mean, gone?" Letti asked. She let go of his chin and sat down on the floor next to him. "You don't mean like Nat?" she said sharply.

Ben looked at her and shook his head. "No, not that. He's left to join up."

"That makes two of us who've lost someone, then. You can tell me, if you want to, Ben," Letti said.

Shame that he had forgotten Nat's recent death overcame Ben. He told her about Zack and about Tarrytown. "It's not that I don't like Aunt Hett's house, but it ain't the same as before," Ben said. "Everything's changed. Now Zack is gone, too."

Letti was silent for a moment. "When Nat and me were little, stealing and looking out for ourselves was all we knew about. After I went to the mission I started changing, and Nat didn't like it. You know the rest," Letti said. "But what if your pa hadn't come here? What if you and Zack hadn't been here to find Nat, or Colin, either? What I'm trying to say," she went on, "is that we can't see where the road goes sometimes, and it can get real hard, but like your ma says, we don't have to make it on our own."

Ben didn't say anything.

Letti put a motherly hand on his shoulder. "You listen to me, Ben. Maybe right now you're missing Zack and wanting to go back to your own house, but all of us got to face the hard parts when they come. It's part of growing." Letti gripped his shoulder harder. "I ain't never gonna forget what you and your pa done for Nat and me. Zack, too. He'll be a fine soldier one of these days. Will you come on now?" she asked. She got to her feet.

Ben lifted his head. "I'll be along in a minute," he said. Letti nodded and left. He would have a lot of explaining to do when Zack didn't show up for dinner. Meanwhile, he needed to sort things out. For an hour Ben sat where he was. At last a kind of wry smile played around his mouth. His mind was made up.

When Ben's father came home for the midday meal, Ben was waiting for him by the front door. "There's something I need to tell you, Pa," he said.

Without a word Ben's father drew him into the privacy of the sitting room and shut the door.

As Ben finished telling his father about Zack and his own anger over the church board's decision, he said, "But I don't feel that way now, honest." He heard himself use Letti's words. "We all have to face the hard times. I guess it's part of growing."

His father's blue eyes looked deeply into Ben's. "Son, I hope you'll forgive me for not seeing what this move meant for you and Zack." He drew Ben to him. "My own heart is breaking for the friends we leave behind." After a moment he said, "But there is one thing I've learned along the way. The Lord never leaves us alone, and his plans for us are good. I'm here for you, son, to remind us both when the going's rough that up ahead good is waiting. As for Zack, we'll do what we can, son."

To Ben's shock, his father said nothing about bringing Zack back. A still greater surprise greeted Ben that evening. In his hand Uncle Hiram held a telegraph. "It seems one of our boys has fallen in with Chaplain Turner himself. This is a message from the chaplain telling us that if no one comes forward to dispute the plan, he will personally take Zack under his wing." Uncle Hiram smiled broadly.

"Thank heaven for that!" Ben's father exclaimed.

Aunt Hett gasped. "Why, I never!"

"Now, Mother," Ben's uncle said, "the boy couldn't be under a finer tutor anywhere than Chaplain Turner."

"He'll be sorley missed," Ben's mother said softly. "I feel like he is one of my own." Looking to her husband for support, she said, "All the same, Stewart, I believe Hiram's right."

Ben knew it was true. A worry had slipped off his shoulders. Zack would be safe with the chaplain.

Abigail cleared her throat loudly, and all eyes turned to her. "If you can bear another announcement, Letti has something to say." Abigail turned to Letti. "Go on," she urged. "This is as good a time as any."

Letti's face turned red as she looked around at the family. Her eyes lingered on Aunt Hett and then on Uncle Hiram. "You all know I been happy here till the trouble with Nat. And you know Captain Sikes offered me a place in his house that I ain't taking," she hurried to add. "Only I am going. Abigail and me, we talked it over. It's something I got to do."

Ben stared. Only last night he had heard those words from Zack. Now he could hear the eagerness in Letti's voice.

"Mr. Thurston says his sister out west wants somebody just like me to help with the children that don't get picked," she said. "I mean the ones the mission sends out on the orphan train and nobody wants them. I'll be learning from Miss Thurston, going to school, and someday maybe teaching on my own." Letti paused before she said quietly, "I think Nat would be pleased. I guess I'll be going with the next orphan train, so long as nobody minds."

Aunt Hett beamed in spite of her tears spilling over. Ben's mother rose and hugged Letti. Over his mother's shoulder Letti winked at Ben. Abigail stood by smiling through her tears.

Something in Letti's face made Ben think of Colin. What was it Zack said about Colin having spunk? Letti had that same kind of courage. Zack too.

"Lass," Uncle Hiram said, patting Letti's head, "you will go with our blessing."

"Up ahead the good is waiting, child," Ben's father added softly.

Only Ben had not yet said a word to Letti. He looked at Letti, the girl from Five Points. Her face glowed and her eyes sparkled with eagerness. All at once he knew that she had given him something he would never forget. "Guess it's all part of growing," he said to remind her of her own words to him. "I'm thinking you will do just fine, Letti."